The Essential Charlotte

Also by Libby Schmais

The Perfect Elizabeth

The *Essential* Charlotte

LIBBY SCHMAIS

Thomas Dunne Books St. Martin's Press ✖ *New York*

THOMAS DUNNE BOOKS.
An imprint of St. Martin's Press.

THE ESSENTIAL CHARLOTTE. Copyright © 2003 by Libby Schmais. All rights reserved.
Printed in the United States of America. No part of this book may be used or
reproduced in any manner whatsoever without written permission except in the
case of brief quotations embodied in critical articles or reviews. For information,
address St. Martin's Press, 175 Fifth Avenue, New York, N.Y. 10010.

www.stmartins.com

Grateful acknowledgment is made to the following for permission to reprint pre-
viously published material:

Excerpt from *Summer and Smoke* by Tennessee Williams, from *The Theatre of Tennessee Williams*, Volume 2. Copyright © 1971 by The University of the South.
Reprinted by permission of New Directions Publishing Corp.

Excerpt from "Just in Time" by Betty Comden, Adolph Green, and Jule Styne.
Copyright © 1956 by Betty Comden, Adolph Green, and Jule Styne. Copyright
renewed. Publication and Allied Rights Assigned to Stratford Music Corporation
and Administered by Chappell & Co. All Rights Reserved. Used by Permission.
Warner Bros. Publications U.S. Inc., Miami, FL 33014.

Design by Susan Yang

Library of Congress Cataloging-in-Publication Data

Schmais, Libby.
    The essential Charlotte / Libby Schmais.—1st ed.
        p. cm.
    ISBN 0-312-31164-8
        1. Inheritance and succession—Fiction. 2. Women medical scientists—
Fiction. 3. Single women—Fiction. 4. Birthfathers—Fiction. 5. Herbalists—
Fiction. 6. Lofts—Fiction. I. Title.

PS3569.C51515E85 2003
813'.6—dc21

                                                                2003040613

First Edition: July 2003

10 9 8 7 6 5 4 3 2 1

To my parents

Acknowledgments

I would like to thank all the people who encouraged and helped me with this book: my agent, Neeti; my editor, Sally; and my loyal manuscript readers, Beth, David, Debbie, and Sam. I would like to thank Liz, who helped me with a difficult scene, and Paula, who read a very early draft. I am eternally grateful to Sam for all his help and insight. I am also deeply indebted to Mina for our weekly writing dates and her unflagging support for this project.

The Essential Charlotte

For times of extreme stress, Ask the Doctor recommends taking a few drops of Rescue Remedy under the tongue. Carry a small bottle with you at all times.

Chapter One

CHARLOTTE WOULD HAVE cried during the funeral service except for her mother's voice in her ear, nudging her to pull herself together, sit up straight, embrace life. The first time she heard the familiar deep voice, she wondered if she was going crazy.

Come on, Charlotte, get it together, you're my representative.

Charlotte knew she should feel sad. After all, this was her mother lying in the funeral parlor. Her mother had always insisted on being called Corinne, even by her daughter. Surprising everyone, she had left instructions for a traditional Catholic service. Although Corinne was technically half Jewish, half Catholic, she had been a devout atheist all her life, aside from a brief flirtation with Buddhism and a cult or two. But for this final performance, she must have decided that the old-fashioned Catholic service, with its incense and Latin words, was the most dramatic.

I'm an orphan now, thought Charlotte. No matter how old you are, when your parents are gone, you are alone—an orphan. Char-

lotte was thirty-three, the same age as Christ when he was cruci-
fied. I am an orphan, Charlotte repeated to herself. She found the
word strangely comforting. It reminded her of her favorite book as
a child, *A Little Princess,* in which young Sara Crewe, motherless
and believing her father dead, is forced into a life of humiliation at
a rich girls' school. She is moved from her luxury suite up into the
decrepit attic, where she is forced to do menial tasks and eat old
crusts of bread. As a child, Charlotte used to imagine facing all
sorts of indignities, with all the courage of little Sara Crewe.

Don't be maudlin, Charlotte, came the unmistakable voice of her
mother, much too close for comfort. Charlotte looked over warily
into the velvety darkness of the closed coffin, half expecting to see
her mother stride out of it in her favorite black suede boots, as if
this whole funeral were a new kind of performance art. She looked
around to see if anyone else was hearing what she was hearing, but
they were all bent over their prayer books, attempting to look
somber.

If she had tried, her mother couldn't have orchestrated a more
theatrical exit, crushed by her own sculpture, a jagged monstrosity
whose price had risen astronomically since her death. A whole ret-
rospective was at this moment being planned at the Guggenheim
Museum.

Actually, the sculpture didn't kill her, as everyone believed. It
was her heart. The medical examiner wrote the cause of death as *a
sudden cardiac event.* What actually occurred was that at the exact
moment her heart stopped beating, Corinne had fallen between the
two looping figures of her latest sculpture.

Her mother was known for huge abstract metal sculptures.
Although listed in the catalogue simply as 17 or 23, at certain
angles they all looked like the interlocking limbs of sexually

ambiguous participants. Charlotte would admire them dutifully but couldn't help feeling vaguely repelled by them.

I'm an orphan now, Charlotte thought, touching the soft leather of the prayer book. Her mother was never very clear on the issue of paternity. When pushed, Corinne would say he was dead, but Charlotte didn't want to believe her. Sometimes, it was difficult for her to believe that she had ever had a father, that her mother hadn't hatched her in the studio from sheer creative force of will. Charlotte used to imagine her father sweeping in to rescue her. *Charlotte is too delicate for this bohemian existence,* he would say. *I'm taking her to my castle in Austria.*

When she used to ask her mother about him, Corinne would say, "It's too painful to talk about, Charlotte," with an eloquent sigh that made Charlotte think Corinne could have succeeded at a career onstage. "I loved your father, but now he is gone. We are alone in the world, you and I."

The reality was they were hardly ever alone. Friends dropped by the loft at all hours of the day or night, smoking Galoises, ordering out bad pizza and consuming endless jugs of red wine. Charlotte would be exhibited at bedtime like a piece of sculpture. She always felt like an early, rather unsuccessful, work.

As the funeral drew to a close, her mother's agent and best friend, Tanya, grabbed her arm.

"We're all going for a drink—Charlotte, you simply must come. I won't take no for an answer."

Charlotte protested, "I really think I need to go home."

"Don't be ridiculous. You need to mourn, Charlotte. This will be a catharsis."

Charlotte shook her head, but the woman wouldn't let go of her arm. She finally unhooked Tanya's clawlike hand and tried to head for the door, but people kept stopping her, saying her name, touching her, sighing, breathing on her, pulling her along with them onto the street. The last thing Charlotte wanted was to go to the Spring Bar, but what she wanted didn't seem to enter into it anymore. So she let go of her free will and let herself be led. Into a cab. Into the bar.

When she got there, it was like an opening for a new exhibit. Bloody Marys and Chardonnays (and cranberry spritzers for the alcoholics) were being passed around freely, people were jostling to get their favorite seats at the bar and air-kissing each other with relief at still being alive and back in their element. Every once in a while, each small group would come to a standstill and lose their train of thought and remember why they were there, but it was only for an instant, and then everything was back to normal. They would call for another drink, more bar snacks, start trashing a critic. People told stories about Corinne: "Remember the time when she threw that vase at Robert . . . got drunk and passed out . . . belly danced on the railing of that apartment?"

Charlotte was sitting at the bar on an uncomfortable tall stool with a hard, slippery seat. She sipped her peppery Bloody Mary, her feet dangling above the floor like a child's, trying to remember the names of all her mother's friends. There was Elaine, obnoxious friend and hanger-on, and Tanya, Corinne's agent from hell. But who was that woman standing right in front of her, the one who always wore those incredibly ugly scarves (today a mustardy geometric pattern)? What was the point of scarves anyway? They were like cigars for women. The uglier the woman, the bigger the scarf. Then, of course, there were the artists: Stan, heavy and sloppy, who painted delicate medieval looking portraits; that girl with the severe bangs who did the tiny dioramas with mutilated troll dolls; all the sculptors. As a child, Charlotte had been dragged to more galleries than she could remember. She always stood in a corner trying to look inconspicuous, so no one would come over and ask her what she thought of the artwork.

Now people kept coming over to her to tell her how wonderful her mother was, what a presence. What an artist. What a loss.

Charlotte felt like she couldn't breathe. People kept hugging her, she had lipstick smeared on her dress, her mother was dead and she just wanted to go home. She got up to leave, but people kept putting their hands on her arm, telling her to stay, to relax, how sad they were, giving her drinks and tiny Japanese crackers.

Charlotte closed her eyes and saw her mother's face. She wondered if her mother had died instantly, or if she had had one of those slow-motion movie moments when her life passed before her eyes, a line of paintings, men (perhaps Charlotte's father), sculptures and then glorious white light. Death. How are you supposed to comprehend that? Corinne existed in the world in one moment and then—boom—gone. There must be another explanation. After all, it was an impossibility that her mother's ferocious energy could have totally disappeared from the world. She was probably right now being channeled into some unsuspecting newborn.

Charlotte, you know I don't believe in the concept of past lives.

There it was again. That voice. "Stop it," Charlotte whispered.

"Charlotte, are you okay?" Her ex-stepfather Kenneth was leaning over her, looking concerned.

"I'm fine," said Charlotte, taking a long sip of her drink, relieved to see someone alive, someone normal.

He frowned. "You looked like you were talking to someone."

"No, I was just thinking out loud."

Her stepfather nodded, crumpling a little inside his tweed jacket. "I know. It's unbelievable—your mother—"

Other people grabbed him away, and Charlotte excused herself to go to the ladies' room. She looked in the mirror for a long time, the way people do after the first time they have sex, to see if they've changed, whether they have achieved a new look of maturity. This is what I look like without a mother, thought Charlotte. Exactly the same.

She stared in the mirror, feeling very far away from the reflection in the glass, as if the woman staring back at her with brown hair and the beginning of fine lines around her eyes were familiar, but she couldn't quite place her. She began to feel dizzy, and sat down on the tiny toilet seat, resting her forehead in her hands. Ordinarily, she would never sit down in a public bathroom, but she remembered reading somewhere that there were more germs on the average office phone than on an average toilet seat. It was hard to believe. She contemplated staying in the tiny metal stall forever, where it was safe and peaceful.

At the edge of her awareness, Charlotte heard someone knocking on the door. She called, "I'll be right out," and got to her feet slowly and carefully, like someone afraid of breaking a hip. She splashed cold water on her face a few times and then flushed the toilet for effect.

Charlotte opened the door warily, ready to apologize to the person waiting, but to her relief there was no one there. She felt cooler and calmer, less like she was going crazy. Her mother wasn't really talking to her; it was just an auditory hallucination. She was going to be fine. She just needed to go home and lie down.

On the way back from the bathroom, she saw a red exit sign and she snuck out the back door of the restaurant, breathing in big gulps of the thick New York City summer air. She ran to the subway entrance and down the stairs as if someone was chasing her, jumping on the train that was just roaring into the station.

She picked up a three-week-old *Village Voice* on the seat next to her and read it from cover to cover on the ride home until her fingers were black with the cheap ink. Movies, political rants, rap music, she read the whole thing, not retaining anything but a vague curiosity about certain abbreviations for sexual practices in the personal ads.

When the train emerged from the tunnel like a giant earthworm, Charlotte saw the pinkish light surrounding the Manhattan skyline from Queens and took her first relaxed breath all day. She was home. Not in Soho, where she had grown up, but in Queens, the home she had adopted. She liked to think that real people lived in her neighborhood, working people, not pale insubstantial artists flitting around galleries like bats. She liked all the tacky fast-food establishments and discount stores lining the street on the way to her apartment, even if she never frequented them. There was a Dunkin' Donuts, a Kentucky Fried Chicken and a clothing store that displayed flowery housedresses proudly in its window.

Her answering machine was blinking frantically when she got inside, but she switched it off and unplugged the phone, yanking the cord out of the wall as hard as she could. She felt drained and shaky and overwhelmed by an urge to get away from her life. Do something different. Move to an exotic island off the coast of India, become a tennis pro, keep bees.

Charlotte walked around the living room, not knowing what to do with herself. What are you supposed to do when your mother has died under an enormous modern sculpture with jagged edges? Her mother had been putting the finishing touches on a large new sculpture, No. 17 of the D series, a series she had been working on for over twenty years. Charlotte had always called it the Dalmatian series because the black metal had white markings that looked like spots. Her mother hated her naming the sculpture. *Stop anthropomorphizing the art, Charlotte,* she used to say.

Charlotte knew her mother had always loved her, but she had loved her in a distant, friendly way. It was nothing like mothers on TV, or the smothering, overprotective mothers of some of her friends. When she was little, Charlotte hardly ever saw her mother. Corinne was always dashing off to openings or theater events or love affairs, leaving Charlotte in the care of her babysitter, Mrs. Marsh, an older woman whom Charlotte adored for her solid presence and her late-night toasted pound cake snacks, dripping with butter.

Charlotte took off her black dress carefully and hung it in her closet. Then, still in her slip, she slowly put on her ballet slippers. She imagined the comforting voice of her ballet teacher and began her ballet exercises, holding on to the molding of her living room wall like a barre. She tried to repeat the familiar words.

"Tendu. Jeté." She lifted her leg up slowly to the three different heights. One day, a little girl watching the ballet class had said that the extensions were like a family: Tendu was the baby, Jeté was the mommy and Grand Battement was the daddy. "Tendu. Jeté.

Grande battement," she whispered, tears running down her face, dripping down onto her slip.

☙

The dance studio was on the Upper East Side, and she had gone to the first ballet class a few months ago, by mistake, thinking she was at her regular stretch class taught by Olga, a tiny Russian. When Olga started barking out positions—"First and fifth and first and fifth"—she had had to peer at the girl standing next to her to figure out how to place her legs and feet. She would have left, but she didn't want to draw attention to herself.

At the end of class she felt exhilarated but clumsy. Ballet was probably not for her. But Olga tracked her down on the way out, touching her shoulder gently. "You should keep coming, you have a natural grace."

So now, when she felt particularly hopeless, she would put on her pink ballet slippers and twirl on the linoleum of her kitchen, murmuring to herself, "I have a natural grace."

☙

Charlotte didn't go to work on Friday, the day after the funeral. She worked for Ask the Doctor, a medical research company. They had a small consumer library, and a few people trickled in now and then to ask questions in person, but most of her work was on the computer, searching distant databases for pharmaceutical information and clinical trials. She e-mailed Paul, her boss and friend:

> Paul,
> My mother died suddenly. I won't be able to come in to work today. I'll be in on Monday.
>
> > Charlotte

He e-mailed her back:

> Charlotte,
> I'm so sorry about your mother . . . if you need to talk . . .
> you know where to reach me.
> Take as much time as you need, sweetie.
> Don't worry about a thing.
>
> Paul

Charlotte had never seen Paul, who worked in the San Francisco office. They communicated over channels, e-mail, voice mail and the occasional telephone call. Paul always called her doll or pumpkin, terms she ordinarily would have found offensive, but she figured it was okay from Paul, whom she pictured as chubby and jovial and definitely gay.

Charlotte sometimes felt as if she were in an episode of *Charlie's Angels,* the old TV show, not the movie, although she couldn't figure out which Angel she would be. She wasn't sexy enough to be the Farrah Fawcett one, or sultry enough to be Jaclyn Smith, so she'd probably have to be the sensible one, the one who always had to get the other two out of trouble. Charlotte even looked a little like Kate Jackson with her dark pageboy, but she wasn't as sinewy.

Ask the Doctor's clients were an eclectic bunch, wealthy hypochondriacs, ad agencies investigating new drug campaigns, even doctors who, before they went on talk shows, wanted a short blurb so they could sound knowledgeable on their subject of expertise. Charlotte's hobby was natural medicine and Ask the Doctor had a web page where Paul let her post a weekly suggestion.

People who knew her well found it ironic that Charlotte worked in the medical field because she was such an incurable hypochondriac and had, on several occasions, thought she was dying of various ailments. As a young child, she had refused, on principle, to use public bathrooms.

"I'll wait until we get home," Charlotte would tell her mother calmly.

Corinne, healthy as a horse, would sigh deeply, as if wondering how they could possibly be related.

"You know, Charlotte, germs can't live on public toilet seats. It's perfectly safe. The twins have no problem with them."

After a while, they began to call her Charlotte the Camel and the twins would time how long she could hold it in.

The twins were her stepsisters. When she was a teenager, they had lived with Corinne and Charlotte on and off for five years. They came with their father, Kenneth, who had married Corinne one afternoon down at City Hall and wrote books so intellectual no one ever seemed to read them. Their mother lived in Europe and didn't seem particularly interested in custody or in the twins, although she doted on Tyler, their older brother. After Kenneth and Corinne split up, the twins stayed on for three more years, and Charlotte moved out to Queens.

If anyone was unconcerned with germs it was her stepsisters, Sophia and Lauren, the twins. It was as if their early proximity in utero had cured them of all fussiness. They would change anywhere, sit anywhere, share bath towels and underwear.

Her mother's theory about germs was that one had to ingest and touch as many as possible in order to build up a healthy immunity. When Charlotte's sandwich fell on the floor, Corinne would pick it up and dust it off, offering it back to Charlotte. "It's perfectly fine," she would assure her, taking a bite. "Dee-licious."

As a child, Charlotte suffered from allergies and inexplicable maladies, closely resembling the ailments of whoever's biography she was reading at the time. At the age of twelve, after devouring a series of books about Chopin, whom she found wonderfully romantic and tragic, Charlotte would carry snowy white handkerchiefs everywhere she went, coughing weakly and pretending to play the piano on the kitchen table.

People always thought that Charlotte should be an artist or writer, because of her mother.

"At least a poet," they would say, as if that were better than nothing, but she had no leanings in an artistic direction, regardless of her parentage. Cool, hard facts were her comforts. Finding an answer to a question. Tracking down a citation.

Because of her fascination with illness, Charlotte didn't find it strange that she was in the medical research profession. As a child, she had collected the entire Sue Barton visiting nurse series, imagining herself as the heroine of each book, and while she didn't feel cut out to be on the front lines with the doctors and nurses and the blood, she could help those as obsessed with medical details as she was.

Charlotte lay back down on her bed, just for a moment. She thought about her mother, the coffin, heard the organ music resounding in her head. When she was a little girl, her mother had told her there was no God, but Charlotte always hoped that she was wrong. Charlotte didn't believe in God, but sometimes, late at night, in the twilight between being awake and being asleep, she had the feeling that some spirit was trying to believe in her. She would feel a warmth, a presence, as if someone was trying to communicate with her, telling her that everything was going to be okay.

When she went to Italy several years ago on a heavily scheduled Cooks tour, Charlotte anointed herself with holy water in churches all through Tuscany, just in case. Although she wasn't brought up Catholic and had to look at the other people to see which hand to cross herself with, no one seemed to mind.

Charlotte told herself that she just needed to rest her eyes, that she wasn't going to go to sleep.

⁕

When she woke up, she felt disoriented. She looked at the clock. It was 5:35 in the afternoon. She got up, went into the kitchen, got the coffee out of the freezer, put it down on the counter and started scooping it out into a new biodegradable coffee filter, but then saw the full pot of coffee that she had made when she got up, staring at her. She walked back into the bathroom. Remedies flowed through her mind.

> Valerian for stress.
> St. John's wort is a natural antidepressant.
> Eat carbohydrates.
> Drink warm milk.

When she went outside to get the mail, there was already a flurry of thick white envelopes. Looking at the envelopes, she could almost imagine she had suddenly gotten popular and was getting invited to fancy dress balls and royal weddings.

Charlotte didn't open the envelopes, after the first few. *So sorry for your loss. Please accept my sincerest condolences.* All the words seemed wooden, meaningless. Corinne had believed that cards were a failing of the lower classes, an attempt to seem refined. *Never send thank-you cards,* she had instructed Charlotte. *Only send invitations, the rest is drivel.*

Charlotte had always sent thank-you cards, believing that her mother was wrong about proper etiquette and not wanting to disappoint, but now the sight of the white envelopes invoked a deep dread in her. If she didn't open them, she wouldn't have to write back. If she didn't open them, none of this would be real.

✾

Saturday was a blur. On Sunday, she decided to go to ballet class. No one there knew about her mother. They only knew Charlotte as the quiet woman who stood in the back of the class, the one with the not-particularly-impressive turnout.

Today, as usual, everyone was talking during class, about ballerinas and eating disorders, and Charlotte lay down on the floor and let the conversation wash over her. When Olga, the teacher, put her hands gently on her back during a stretch, Charlotte clenched her teeth so she wouldn't cry.

Charlotte loved the studio, although she wasn't part of the inner circle, the small group of women who had been coming to ballet forever. Charlotte envied them their faded leotards and tights with holes, and their easy banter with Olga, who ran the studio with her husband, Klaus.

Most of the people who took class were in the "entertainment business," which could mean anything from a serious opera tour through Europe to occasionally playing a maiden at a Renaissance fair in Ohio. Still, to Charlotte they seemed to be glamorous representatives from the world of theater. During the ending stretches, a petite girl who had obviously been taking ballet for years made an announcement.

"I'm looking for some people to be in this production I'm doing. It's nonequity."

The room filled with sighs.

"And it doesn't pay."

More sighs.

"Come on, I'm desperate. It's going to be a lot of fun."

"What is it?" asked a bored girl who wore leotards cut very low in the back, showing off her bony spine.

"*Medea.*"

Olga tiptoed her way to the front of the room. "Okay, everyone at the barre, we are going to work on positions. En croix. What does that mean?" she asked, like a grade school teacher.

"On the cross," replied Dana, Olga's best friend, who was always in class, bringing her coffee, gossiping about mutual acquaintances, laughing at her jokes. They were like one of those late-night talk show teams, the host and the reliable sidekick.

Olga replied, as she always did, "En croix, that's for us Catholics. Front, side, back, side, for everyone else."

Once the girl said the play wasn't equity and it wasn't going to pay, everyone seemed to have lost interest. But all during class, through the tendus and jetés, Charlotte imagined herself playing Medea. A tragic figure. Wearing a long red velvet dress.

⁂

On Monday, Charlotte got to work early. It was a relief to get back to her normal routine. First she read the health and science sections of the papers, the entire *New York Times,* and then skimmed through various health newsletters and medical journals. She clipped an article on floods for Tom, one of the regulars. Although the small library was a consumer health library, he came once a week like clockwork to read about disasters, on the Internet. His latest theory was that the entire Northeast would be submerged in water by 2015 after being hit by an asteroid.

"Houseboats," he had told Charlotte sotto voce the other day, as if the other library patrons were going to run out and scoop up all the remaining floor models, "that's the answer."

Every few weeks he would bring her a package of dehydrated flakes, which he claimed would reconstitute into a delicious meal.

"Chili," he whispered the other day, pressing a shiny new package into her hand like an experienced drug dealer.

She filed the packets in a folder she had set up labeled DISASTER.

Charlotte often had to deal with strange problems. Once, an elderly woman came up to her and unbuttoned her own blouse, exposing a complicated white bra that looked like a straitjacket, in order to show Charlotte a small brown mole.

"Is it a melanoma? I read about a swimsuit model who had that, in *Woman's Day*."

"Mrs. Kleinman," Charlotte had said gently, "this is a library, not a hospital. Button up your shirt."

"I don't want to go to the doctor, he's a big know-nothing. Managed care." She sniffed. "He wouldn't know how to manage a checkbook."

How can you deal with all those sniveling hypochondriacs?

"Be quiet," hissed Charlotte, hoping no one would hear.

Her stepsisters called her on Thursday, exactly a week after the funeral. They were only three years older than Charlotte, but were always telling her what to do and giving her unsolicited advice.

"We would have been there, but the trip was nonrefundable. Corinne probably would have wanted us to go."

"To the funeral?"

"No, to Hawaii. You know how she was always saying to live for the moment."

Why was it that when people were dead, everyone becomes an expert on what they would have wanted? Of course, they were probably right, Corinne was always extremely indulgent of her stepchildren, slipping them twenties and telling them to go out and have a good time. If they didn't do their homework or try hard enough, they were never reprimanded. Charlotte, on the other hand, got all As and no one ever noticed.

Having entered their lives during an affluent period of Corinne's, the twins became very attached to her, not to mention to the idea of living in Soho and having meals prepared by the housekeeper. Although the twins were older than Charlotte, they had a youthful kind of gaiety about them. They worked at an investment bank, wore very short skirts and clunky high heels and were always looking for the next party. Charlotte's most vivid memory of the period when they all lived together were the clouds of glittering powder, the shiny pots of mysterious makeup, the hour and a half it took them to get ready to go anywhere. It was hard to believe they were only fourteen at the time.

"You need to get out," they said simultaneously and arranged to have dinner with Charlotte on Friday night. They lived together, finished each other's thoughts, borrowed each other's clothes, although Sophia, the younger of the two by a matter of minutes, looked better in them. They reminded Charlotte of tiny chattering birds.

<hr/>

It was pouring rain when Charlotte locked the door to the Ask the Doctor library for the week, raining so hard that she started to believe Tom's dire predictions about the end of the world. She took a cab to meet her stepsisters at a new Italian place in the Village they had heard of—Risotteria. Ordering food was always very complex with the twins. They were perpetually on a diet, so dinner involved splitting many dishes so they wouldn't miss out on anything, yet could feel that they weren't really eating.

There were two types of people, thought Charlotte, watching the twins twitter and peck at mounds of rice: those who feel that wherever they are is where the party is, and those, like herself, who feel that wherever they are, the party is happening elsewhere.

Her mother and the twins were the first type. No matter how much Charlotte hated Corinne for marrying and divorcing stepfathers and generally being unavailable, Charlotte always had the feeling that when her mother was present, something elemental was happening.

"Earth to Charlotte," said Lauren. "Did you hear me? Are you going to the reading of the will next week? Did that fossil call you?"

"Mr. Sneed is not a fossil," said Charlotte indignantly, although as she pictured her mother's ancient lawyer in her mind, she realized the description was apt. "He's just well preserved." She started laughing and Lauren and Sophia joined in, pausing for a moment from poking their forks into her risotto.

"Did he call you?" persisted Lauren. "Aren't you curious?"

"He left a couple of messages on my machine. I guess he wants me to call him. I don't know." Charlotte sighed. She felt exhausted at the thought of dealing with her mother's legal affairs.

"You have to go, Charlotte. This is important. It's next Wednesday, at four," said Lauren.

"Yes," agreed Sophia, who corrected anyone who tried to call her that. "My name is Sophie," she had told Charlotte the first time they met. "I mean, Sophia and Lauren, what the hell were they thinking."

*For mental and physical exhaustion caused by illness or
personal ordeals, Olive assists in giving strength and vitality.*

Chapter Two

CHARLOTTE WALKED SLOWLY down the long hallway of the
Midtown law firm, her sensible leather pumps sinking into
the heavily carpeted floor. She longed for Jules, her best
friend since college. When she heard about her mother, Charlotte
had immediately picked up the phone to call Jules, realizing as
the phone rang and rang that Jules was hiking in the Costa
Rican rain forest. Jules was a travel writer and she was always off
in some exotic place. Charlotte had even called the travel agent
who booked the trip, but there was absolutely no way to reach
her.

"Totally incommunicado," the woman had said in a hushed
tone that could have worked in a James Bond film. "Deep in the
rain forest."

Jules had invited Charlotte to go with her, but Charlotte had
pictured large Costa Rican bugs and no indoor plumbing, not to
mention the fact that you couldn't wash your hair for three weeks.
Now she wondered if she should have gone with Jules. Would it

have changed anything? Could one tiny change of plans have unraveled history and kept her mother alive?

Charlotte stopped walking for a moment in front of the Poland Spring water cooler and had a drink of water in a conical paper cup. Men in suits were striding purposefully past her, rustling bunches of paper and files, and the Poland Spring song was echoing in her mind.

Mr. Sneed's firm was considered a "white shoe" firm, where only attorneys of the most patrician backgrounds were acceptable. Her mother had always been impressed with prestige, and while she would skimp on almost anything—food, clothes, wine—she insisted on having the oldest, most conservative law firm and the oldest, most crumbling lawyer represent her.

"My retainer," she liked to say, as if she were in a Charles Dickens novel.

The will had been hanging over Charlotte's head for so long, she was probably going to miss it after today. In maudlin red wine moments, her mother would claim to be totally alone in the world and threaten to cut everyone out of the will, all the ex-lovers, the ungrateful friends, the disappearing twins.

"I'll cut them all out, the bloodsuckers," she would hiss. Even Charlotte was excised from the will on these occasions. "It would do you good, Charlotte, to be out on your own, no velvet cushion to fall back on." Corinne didn't see any inconsistency in talking about her will even during pretwin times when they barely had enough money to buy groceries. She had total confidence in her posthumous value. Charlotte was embarrassed but not upset by this kind of tirade. The things she had always wanted from Corinne weren't as simple as money.

"Tea, Charlotte?" inquired Mr. Sneed, after she finished the long journey down the hallway to the corner office where he presided. "Or would you rather have something more bracing?"

"Tea would be lovely, Mr. Sneed. Thanks."

Mr. Sneed was thin, with fading white hair and an ever-present paisley bow tie. He moved silently, smelled like cloves and had an improbable fondness for modern art. His office was cluttered with large abstract paintings and Victoriana. He had always been extremely kind to Charlotte, and at a young age she had wanted him to adopt her. Recently, she had been sending him herbal remedies for his various conditions.

Appearing beside her suddenly with a delicate china cup, he murmured, "I haven't had the opportunity to convey how deeply sorry I was to hear of your mother's demise, although I believe she would have wanted it this way, to go in the line of duty, so to speak."

Charlotte nodded at Mr. Sneed as she tried to get comfortable on her feeble tapestry chair and balance her cup of Lapsang souchong—no easy feat. She didn't particularly like the flavor of the smoky tea but she liked the sound of it. Lap. Song. Soo. Chong. She remembered lying on Mr. Sneed's Oriental rug as a small child, while her mother dealt with numerous lawsuits and divorce actions, playing with legal books, the spicy smell of the tea pervading the office as Charlotte made mountains of all the Martindale Hubbells and Second Circuit decisions.

"So, how are you feeling, Mr. Sneed? How's the gout?"

"Such a ridiculous disease. I tried the ice packs and the cherries you suggested. They do seem to be helping a little."

"Good."

"Charlotte, there's something I wanted to discuss before the others arrive. I tried to call you several times, but I must have missed you." He cleared his throat. "This is difficult, Charlotte. Your mother contacted me last year and wanted me to track down your father."

"My father?" Charlotte said the words slowly as if this were a scientific concept that she couldn't quite grasp, like a quark or a black hole.

"Yes, your father. At your mother's request, I then hired a private detective, from a very reputable firm, and they undertook a search. Needless to say, it was not a quick process."

"She never said anything about it."

"Your mother was inordinately fond of surprises."

"Why did she want to find him?"

"Your mother had been having episodes—spells, we might have said in my day. She probably didn't want to worry you. Eventually, she went for a series of tests. After they got the results, the doctor— the top cardiologist at Mount Sinai, to be precise—told your mother that she needed an operation to remove a clot."

Charlotte stared at him. When she received the phone call about her mother's death, she had thought it was just what they said, a sudden heart attack, but now she realized that all her assumptions were wrong, that her mother had known she was ill.

"But I don't understand. What does this have to do with my father? Did you find him?"

❦

Before Mr. Sneed had a chance to continue, she heard her stepsisters barreling down the hallway and into his office. They were dressed in identical knockoff Chanel suits they had draped with numerous gold chains and belts, which were rattling loudly. Their father, her ex-stepfather, trailed behind them, in a sober dark gray suit. During the three years of their marriage, Kenneth never really was able to stop her mother from throwing tantrums, getting drunk or wasting money, but he was a comforting presence to have around the house, just to know he was there, in his study, working on yet another book about socioeconomic policies in the Third World.

Mr. Sneed looked upset that he couldn't finish telling her about her mother. "We'll talk later, Charlotte, I'm sorry."

The twins crossed over to her, kissed the air around her face, and Lauren whispered, "Hey, Charlotte, did Corinne own the loft?"

"Outright?" chimed in Sophie.

"Why?" asked Charlotte, still dazed by what Mr. Sneed had been saying about her mother. An operation could have helped her. Things she had read about heart disease came flooding back to her. Coenzyme Q10. Garlic. Hawthorn berries helped dilate arteries. Guggul is good for lowering cholesterol. Had Corinne even had high cholesterol?

"Just wondering what was going to happen to it."

"Quiet, girls." said Kenneth, and surprisingly, they listened to him. He kissed Charlotte on the cheek and sat down next to her.

"Nice to see you again, Charlotte. How are you holding up?"

"I don't know. I feel like I'm watching a play. I can't really take it in yet. Sometimes I'll pick up the phone and I'll know it's Corinne, but then it never is . . . I can't believe this is happening."

"I know."

They stood there silent for a moment, and then Charlotte started talking, just to fill up all the empty space. "I'm thinking of taking up acting."

"You're not quitting your job, are you?" asked Kenneth. "Because I don't think you'll be in a position—"

"No, it's just something I always wanted to do."

Several prominent-looking people arrived. The twins nudged Charlotte with their bony elbows. "Do you see that woman with the big nose and the cape? I think she's from the Guggenheim."

"They probably want to make sure they got all the sculptures."

After all the new arrivals were settled with glasses of sherry or cups of tea, brought by Mr. Sneed personally or by his young male secretary, everyone waited, some on frail chairs that looked as if they were about to throw their inhabitants headfirst onto the blood-colored carpet. Other people leaned up against bookcases.

Charlotte looked around the room. There were the art vultures, a few friends of her mother and several men she didn't know.

There was a very tanned, leathery man leaning in the corner, wearing a safari jacket in a kind of Robert Redford way. Charlotte pegged him as a former lover. There was also a chubby French-looking man who didn't seem to fit in. Either former lover or art critic, Charlotte couldn't decide which.

"Listen to Mr. Sneed, girls, it's starting," said their father.

"I, Corinne K. Stiles, of the City, County and State of New York, being of sound mind and body, do make, publish, and declare this to be my last Will and Testament, hereby revoking all wills and codicils at any time heretofore made by me."

While Mr. Sneed droned on through the will, Charlotte conjured up her favorite memory of her mother when she was little. Whenever her mother was home at night—and that wasn't too often, what with openings and men and trips to France—Charlotte would beg to be read to from her favorite books. On the rare occasions when she agreed, her mother would try to read from books that she thought would improve Charlotte's mind, primarily *The Fountainhead,* which was Corinne's personal guide to life, or, failing that, anything from *Anna Karenina* to Anaïs Nin. But Charlotte would always insist on her own two favorite books, either *A Little Princess* or *Charlotte's Web.* Despite her mother's protests that she was named after an obscure French poetess, Charlotte de la Mare, Charlotte was convinced that her mother had named her after the Charlotte in *Charlotte's Web* and made her read through the book, over and over, year after year, whenever her mother felt guilty enough. She loved that book so much. Sometimes she saw herself as Wilbur, the hapless, doomed pig, and sometimes as Charlotte, the wise spider who saves Wilbur and sacrifices all. Mostly, she just wanted to live in that barn, where it was safe and warm, and where there were always scraps of delicious food in Wilbur's pail.

"First: I give and bequeath to my dear friend Rachel (Sacha) Sanchez, if she survives me, all my early sculptures of the A series, in appreciation for her unflagging devotion and promotion of my career.

"I give and bequeath to Kenneth Pollan, for his years of good friendship after our divorce, the sculptures entitled 18 and 19 of the D series."

The will went on and on. There were major and minor bequests. The chubby Frenchman and the safari jacket man both got signed prints and looked smug. The housekeeper, Mrs. Marsh, in her absence (she had retired to Kentucky) got some lithographs. Finally, Mr. Sneed announced a small sculpture going to the twins and they squealed and hugged each other. Several other bequests of sculptures and drawings and personal effects were given to various friends and hangers-on.

Charlotte heard Mr. Sneed's voice from a distance while she was having a fantasy of taking care of her mother, nursing her back from her heart condition, feeding her special low-fat foods, potions and remedies. Charlotte would have been the perfect nurse, unfazed by anything—outbursts, bodily fluids, crises. They would have watched old movies together, her mother's favorites: *Dr. Zhivago, Anne of the Thousand Days, Mildred Pierce.*

"Except as hereinabove effectively bequeathed, I give and bequeath the remains of all my tangible personal property, including, without limitation, my collection of letters, papers and documents, my personal effects, clothing, etc., etc., to my beloved daughter, Charlotte Stiles."

Beloved. *Beloved,* Charlotte thought. Isn't that a Toni Morrison novel?

❦

Mr. Sneed had stopped reading from the will and was looking at Charlotte.

"Charlotte, as you were no doubt aware, you are the primary beneficiary of your mother's estate. Unfortunately, the estate's major assets are the sculptures, and they have been generously donated to the Guggenheim Museum for a special sculpture exhibit organized by Ms. Elena Rambeau, who has graciously joined us here today to represent the museum."

There was a small sprinkling of applause, and Ms. Rambeau and her big nose bowed slightly.

Then Mr. Sneed turned again to Charlotte.

"Charlotte, the other primary asset remaining is the loft, which would be a good way to recoup money into the estate. However, there is a special provision your mother insisted on, against my wishes, might I add. She desires—excuse me, desired—that you reside there. In fact, she insisted on it. All the expenses—that is, property taxes, maintenance and utility bills—will be paid by the estate for the period of one year."

Everyone looked at Charlotte. She felt hot and sweaty. I'm not living there, she thought, memories of dust and red wine making her feel like she was choking. She can't make me. Why does she want me to live in the loft anyway? I'm happy in Queens.

Think you're happy, whispered her mother's voice in her ear.

"There is one more thing. Your mother thought it was about time you got to know your father—that is, your biological father—and to that end, she has left the loft jointly to the both of you, on the condition that you occupy it together for a year before you contemplate any sale."

Biological father. What was he talking about? Then she remembered. The private detective. They must have found him. Why?

"That's absurd," said Kenneth. "We have no way to find this man. He could be dead."

"As it so happens," said Mr. Sneed, a great reader of detective novels, with a flourish of his sherry, "the man is with us here now."

Charlotte's eyes swept over the men in the room. There was no one whom she could look at and think, Yes, this is my father, but there were three or four possibilities: the Frenchman, the safari guy, a hippie who had gotten a small pen-and-ink drawing. No, please not him. It was like one of those Hercule Poirot mysteries she used to read, in which Mr. Sneed, as the dapper Poirot, would be about to twirl his mustache and reveal the identity of the killer.

As she settled her hopes on the tanned man in the safari jacket, Mr. Sneed coughed dramatically.

"This is so exciting," whispered the twins, nudging Charlotte with their elbows.

A man Charlotte hadn't noticed started walking over to her. He looked ordinary: brown hair, khaki pants and loafers. Loafers. How could her father be wearing loafers? All her life she had dreamed of being rescued by her mysterious father, who had been away somewhere killing dragons and saving the world, but now that it was actually happening, she felt nothing but nausea. As a little girl, she had imagined her father as exotic, a dark count in evening wear and shiny black dancing shoes. But how could a man in loafers rescue you? Loafers were the essence of ordinary.

As the man came toward Charlotte, everyone in the room went silent, watching them.

The man started talking.

"Charlotte, I just want to tell you that . . ." He moved closer.

"I have to go," said Charlotte, not even wanting to look at him. She felt nauseous and short of breath. Is this what a heart attack feels like? she wondered.

"Charlotte, please, I need to explain to you."

Charlotte got up from her chair, almost knocking it over. "I don't want to hear it. You're not my father. I don't have a father."

"Charlotte—"

"Get away from me."

Charlotte's goal was to leave the office before she started crying. Luckily, she was near the door. I will not cry. I will not cry. Her stepfather started to come over to her, but she waved him away.

"Charlotte. Please. Wait up," said the man who claimed to be her father, walking toward her. "We need to talk about this."

"Don't bother," said Charlotte, still managing not to cry, as she ran out the door. Not crying past the lawyers, not crying all the way to the elevator, until the doors closed and she started hurtling downward.

⚶

The next morning, Charlotte phoned Mr. Sneed.

"Charlotte, dear, I'm so sorry about yesterday. That wasn't what I intended. To upset you like that."

Charlotte still felt angry, although out loud she said, "Forget it. It doesn't matter."

"I know it must have been a terrible shock, but I thought you would have been happy to meet your father."

"Happy? That some stranger waltzes in and turns my life upside down? No. I'm not happy. And he's not my father."

"I'm sorry, Charlotte, I just meant that—"

"Is there any way to get out of this, to contest the will, legally?"

Mr. Sneed cleared his throat apologetically. "I was afraid you were going to ask me that, so I looked at the will again this morning and did a little research. It really is an unusual request, but there are some precedents and there is nothing actually illegal about the codicil. Frankly, Charlotte, I'm afraid it would be a waste of time and a waste of a great deal of money to attempt any legal procedure to contest it. That's not to say that you aren't free to attempt it. I could recommend some good solicitors."

"You couldn't do it?"

"No, it would be a conflict of interest, you see."

"Of course. You're still her lawyer."

"In a sense. I represent the estate, so I can't represent you against it. But Charlotte, there's something else I'd like you to think about. These were your mother's last wishes. I think you should honor them."

"I know, but what about my wishes? What about my life?"

Mr. Sneed was silent for a moment. "I remember you so distinctly as a little girl, Charlotte, and how you were always reading myths, or 'meeths,' as you used to call them. You were such a serious little girl. I remember one day you asked me if I could adopt you until your father came back."

Charlotte smiled to herself, remembering long afternoons playing on the rug in his office, reading her book of myths. She remembered that day. He hadn't laughed at her and had actually looked very touched in a stuffy Mr. Sneed kind of way.

"Charlotte, I think you owe it to yourself to give this man a chance. His name is William, by the way, William LaViolette. From what I've seen of him, he seems a very nice man."

Wild Oat is the remedy for indecisiveness.

Chapter Three

TWO WEEKS HAD passed since the funeral and Charlotte lay on the cold wooden floor, breathing. Even though they had all been instructed to focus on themselves, she took a peek around at the other beginner acting students lying down near her. There were around twenty other people, a mixed bag of ages and looks. She had been under the mistaken impression that there would only be beautiful people at an acting class, but looking around, she was reassured by the presence of a few decidedly not-so-beautiful types.

A few days before, in a moment of impulsiveness, Charlotte had called the girl from her dance class about getting a part in the play.

"Hi, Jodee, you probably don't remember me, but my name is Charlotte and I'm in your dance class, at Olga's. Do you remember a couple of weeks ago you were talking about a production of

Medea . . . and I thought . . . I mean, I was wondering—"

"Can you hold on a sec?"

Charlotte was deflated, "I'm sorry, is this a bad time?" She twisted and untwisted the telephone cord around her wrist.

"No, it's just my other line is ringing."

Charlotte held on, her finger on the receiver, telling herself she could push the button and hang up at any time.

"Hi. Sorry. You were calling about . . ."

"About the play." She doesn't even remember, Charlotte thought.

"Right, it's just that that show was only for a couple of nights, and it's over. A flop, actually."

"Oh." I shouldn't have called.

"So. . . . Charlotte, is that right?"

"Yes," said Charlotte, finger poised to hang up the phone.

"What else have you been in?"

"Well, nothing, actually. I'm a medical librarian."

Jodee sounded excited. "You know about medical stuff?"

"Yes."

"Do you know anything about the prostate?"

"Well . . ."

"My boyfriend has one."

"Most men do," said Charlotte dryly

"He's been having some problems."

"Oh. Well, I know that saw palmetto berries are supposed to be good for prostate problems."

"Saw palmetto berries. Wow. Look, I know what you should do. Take some acting classes at The Craft. It's incredible."

"Well, I don't know. I'm not—"

"They always cast their students in their showcases. Just show up Monday night. Level one classes are at seven. I'll be there. I should be in the level two classes—but they start at eight in the morning and there is just no way."

☙

The night Charlotte arrived at the class, there was a special orientation about the school. The founder of the school, John Gladstone, who looked exactly like Peter O'Toole, had spoken. He started with a short history of the studio and its two famous alumni, successful actors who wrote and starred in their own gritty dramas. Then he told the students they would start by doing some simple exercises to open them up.

"He teaches the Thursday class," Jodee whispered to Charlotte, "by audition only."

John, as he told them to call him, congratulated them on their choice of school, and told them acting would change their lives, if they let it. He gave them advice in his deep sonorous voice. Told them the rules of the school:

> Take the craft of acting seriously.
> Treat your bodies with respect.
> Treat your fellow actors with respect.
> Always follow your instincts.
> Always make a choice.

He told them about his policy on auditing.

"We don't allow auditing here at The Craft. You see, acting is all about learning to be private in public. People are expressing their inner selves here and they need to be able to trust their fellow actors. You will be dropping your defenses, dropping your poses, sometimes even dropping your pants, so you can see why visitors wouldn't be appropriate." Someone giggled, and he gave them a stern look.

✺

Charlotte let her body sink into the ground. She felt the length of her spine along the floor. She breathed in from her diaphragm up to her collarbone. He must be kidding, she thought. I'm not taking my clothes off. I don't care how prestigious The Craft is.

Don't be such a prude, Charlotte.

✺

The instructor for the level one class was a thin blond woman in her mid-forties named Susan. She was nice but serious. She had two assistants, Sharon and Colin, who roamed the room, placing books on people's stomachs to help with their breathing or putting their hands on areas that seemed tense.

Sharon came by and put a book on Charlotte's stomach. Charlotte whispered, "Thank you," but the girl put her fingers to her lips.

"Just focus on your breathing."

The book was heavy on Charlotte's stomach, a dead weight. Instead of helping her breathe, it made her feel she couldn't breathe at all. She wanted to take it off, but she didn't want to call attention to herself. She concentrated on trying to concentrate on her breathing. She tried to empty her mind. But she kept thinking about her father. He hadn't looked familiar. In books, people always know their long-lost parents by their familiar smell or a warm glowing feeling. Maybe it was a mistake and he wasn't her father at all. Sara Crewe would have known her father anywhere, even though he had amnesia from a head injury and didn't recognize her.

Charlotte felt light all of a sudden. The book had been lifted. She looked up to see who her savior was. It was the other assistant, Colin. He picked up the book, turning the cover over so she could see it—*War and Peace.*

"I've always preferred *Anna Karenina,*" he said, winking at her, then walked away. He had a wonderful melting Irish accent, and Charlotte thought he was one of the most handsome men she had ever seen.

I'll say, said her mother.

Charlotte looked around, but no one had even looked up from their exercise, confirming her suspicion that she was the only one who could hear Corinne.

They did other relaxation exercises. In one, they had to stand with their feet apart and let their heads hang down between their knees.

"Sometimes," Susan said, "you can almost feel your whole body vibrating from the release of emotions. You have to be open to that."

Charlotte only felt dizziness from the rush of blood to her head.

After class, Charlotte met Jules at a fifties-style diner they liked. She felt as if a lifetime had passed since she had seen her friend, not just three weeks. The two were opposites: Jules was tall and curvy with curly blond hair, while Charlotte was thin, olive-skinned, more delicate-looking. In the movie of their lives, Jules would be played by Kate Winslet, Charlotte by Winona Ryder or Kate Beckinsale.

Charlotte was sitting at a booth when Jules rushed in, breathless and twenty minutes late as usual, and gave her friend a long hard hug.

"Sorry I'm late, traffic was hell."

"It's okay, I'm used to it. You look great."

"Thanks. Charlotte, I wish I had known about your mother. I would have cut my trip short. I'm so sorry I wasn't there."

"It's okay. I know you would have."

Jules sat down and they ordered macaroni and cheese, chocolate egg creams and iceberg lettuce salads with blue cheese dressing.

"Should we be extra-decadent and get the Frito pie too?" asked Jules, flagging down the waitress.

"Definitely," said Charlotte, relieved to finally be with her friend.

"I'm stunned about your mother. I just can't believe it. How did it happen?"

"One of those new sculptures she was working on fell on her. But she wasn't crushed. In fact, she looked perfect. They said she must have had a massive coronary as it was falling."

"Wow. It's so hard to believe. She was so alive!"

They sat silent for a few minutes, until the waitress brought their food. Charlotte started to eat her Frito pie, which was a bag of Fritos, slit down the middle, topped with veggie chili and melted cheese. It was incredibly unhealthy and Charlotte usually loved it, but today the smell of the chili was making her feel queasy.

"You know, sometimes I swear I hear her talking to me."

"What does she say?"

"The usual, tells me what to do. Criticizes."

"I suppose I shouldn't say this now, but your mother never liked me."

"It's okay. I think she was jealous. She never really liked any of my friends. She would always try to win them over. And you didn't let her."

"She *was* charming."

"You know what I keep thinking about, Jules? Maybe it's selfish of me to even say it, but she didn't even leave me one sculpture in her will. Not one. Not a painting, not a drawing, not one piece of artwork. People I never heard of got bequests in her will. The twins even got something. And my . . . that man. I can't believe that she never told me. That she did this to me."

"Well, she did leave you the loft."

"With substantial strings attached."

"What are you going to do about that?"

"There is no way I'm living there with that man."

"Okay, okay. Are you going to eat that?" said Jules, pointing to Charlotte's Frito pie.

Charlotte slid it over, along with the rest of her macaroni and cheese.

"Why is it that thin people, like you, can't eat when they're upset, but larger people, like me, eat more when they're stressed?"

"It's because we were all originally hunter-gatherers," said Charlotte. "It's for the survival of the species. If you are thin, your body believes there is a shortage of food and cuts back, but if you have reserves, your body believes there is an abundance and goes for it."

"Reserves, that's a nice way to put it," said Jules, scanning the dessert menu.

Over an ice-cream sundae for Jules and coffee for Charlotte, Charlotte told Jules about the acting class.

"I really like it. I mean, we didn't do any real acting yet, but it's great. You forget about everything. We've been doing breathing exercises and in a couple of weeks we're going to do scenes."

"Any cute guys?"

"Well, there's one, but I'm sure he's taken."

"You never know."

When Jules said goodbye at the subway, Charlotte felt her brief good mood start to dissolve. On the N train back to Astoria, Charlotte was wedged in between the metal door and a bulky woman with a large, pointy backpack that was digging into Charlotte's side. Charlotte wanted to kill her. The woman with the backpack was turned away from her, so Charlotte gave the backpack a gentle shove, but it swung right back into her. The next time, she gave it a good hard push, and when the woman turned around angrily, Charlotte settled an innocent expression on her face and became engrossed in an article in *Herb Research Weekly* on gingko biloba. The woman looked around, but wasn't sure who to get angry at. Charlotte knew how she looked to strangers. Calm, safe, reliable. That was how people always saw her. She could hear her heart pounding in her ears. She forced herself to read the magazine, making a mental note that ginkgo was also a useful treatment for tinnitus.

On her way home, she walked by all her familiar haunts, saying their names out loud as if they were talismans. Greek store. Laundromat. Genovese. Italian deli with the sign for meatball parmesian instead of meatball parmesan. This was where she lived. She wanted to stay here. Outside of Manhattan, the sky became a dark soft blue. She looked up at it, taking a deep breath, and forgot everything for a moment. Then everything came crowding back. She tried to think about the loft so she wouldn't have to think about her "father," although now the two things were inextricably entwined in her mind. She could see the blank spaces and odd shapes of the loft so easily. She didn't want to live there, but it was so tempting. It wasn't sentimental feelings or her mother's wishes that made her consider living there. It was the money. People always thought she and her mother were wealthy, but her mother didn't become famous until ten years or so before her death. When Charlotte was growing up, there was never enough money to go around, and her mother was so nonchalant about it that Charlotte felt she had to worry for both of them.

Later, when she started becoming known, written up, shown, Corinne could have made a fortune, but she hated to part with her sculptures. Occasionally she'd give them away, or sell them to people she liked at reduced prices. When she did get some money, she'd spend most of it on research trips to France or hunks of marble or cashmere shawls that cost a small fortune.

Even now that Charlotte had a regular income and a savings account and had started an IRA (Paul didn't offer a retirement plan), she compulsively wrote up budgets, figuring out how long her money could last if it had to.

But a loft. A large loft. In Soho. Her mother's loft. The loft of a famous sculptress who had died unexpectedly. She could live there for a year, sell it and never have to worry about money again.

On the walk home, it seemed like she only saw parents, men with children, women with children, women kissing and cuddling their infants. Had she ever been that small? Had her mother ever held her like that?

Looking at the families, Charlotte wondered who would take care of her when she was old. She knew she wasn't going to have children. Everyone always said there was plenty of time to meet someone, to have kids, but Charlotte knew she wasn't cut out for that. Too many things could go wrong. Diseases, kidnapping, mutations. She was fine about not having children. Plus, she wasn't getting any younger. Her eggs were probably already in a coma, stale, past their due date.

Jules, on the other hand, was older than Charlotte, thirty-seven, and obsessed with having a child. She was even talking about adopting one on her own if she wasn't in a stable relationship by the time she was thirty-eight. Charlotte couldn't understand wanting to have a child that badly. Children needed so much—so much love, so much attention, so much time. They would swallow her up in their neediness. How could people know with such clarity that they wanted children? Know, without a doubt, that they would be comfortable never being alone again? Or maybe that was exactly why they did it—so they'd never have to be.

From the time Charlotte could remember, she was always taking care of things, taking care of her mother. Her mother had a circuit of people she traveled with and through, getting free places to stay and time to work on her art. She managed to make the people she stayed with feel grateful, as if she were doing them a favor by allowing them to take a brief course in observing an artist. She took Charlotte everywhere, drank too much and then ignored her. It was painting back then, presculpture, prefame, and what Charlotte remembered most about her childhood was the smell of turpentine, her mother's smock covered with blues and greens, the paint-stained brushes everywhere.

At the door to her apartment, she saw her landlady, Mrs. Constantinople. Usually she stopped to chat with her, but she hadn't told Mrs. C about her mother's death and she felt guilty about it. She kept meaning to tell her, but she didn't want to upset the balance of woes, have too many on her side.

"Charlotte, how are you?"

"I'm okay Mrs. C. How are you?"

Mrs. C sighed, a deep loud sigh that seemed to come from the very depths of her being. She wore a housecoat of faded flowers and Nike sneakers. "My son, he comes home at four in the morning last night, and I have to get up at six."

Charlotte shook her head, commiserating. The younger son, Niko, didn't seem to work. The older son was a chiropractor. Niko usually hung out on the stoop, in white nylon shorts and black socks, smoking cigarettes, talking on his cell phone, acting like he was a player.

Mrs. C made her way back into her dark gloomy apartment, patting Charlotte on the shoulder.

"I've got to go cook dinner, you get some sleep. You look terrible."

⁂

Walking upstairs, away from the strange burned-cooking smells of Mrs. C, Charlotte closed the door on the outside world with relief. Inside her apartment, she started mixing up a special formula of Rescue Remedy. In the 1930s, Dr. Edward Bach had postulated that the essences of flowers could cure various emotional problems, and in the year 2003 the idea still appealed to Charlotte. The flowers for the remedies were picked by the light of the moon on certain auspicious nights and diluted until only the hidden vibrational power of the flowers remained. There were flower remedies for a variety of emotional states. At her old job at the public library, Charlotte had taken wild oats for indecisiveness and three weeks later had answered an ad in the *New York Times* for the medical research position with Paul, although she had no relevant medical experience. Rescue Remedy was a special combination of five flower essences to combat emotional shock.

For times of extreme stress, she marked on the label of the dark brown bottle in her careful print. She spilled out a few drops on her tongue, feeling like an addict.

How could she have a father after all this time anyway? After wanting so much to have one? Even if this man really was her biological father, he wasn't her real father. He was just a sperm donor. He didn't have to be a part of her life. She didn't need a father.

She had to distract herself from these thoughts. The Rescue Remedy wasn't working. Even flower essences had their limits. Charlotte fiddled with the bottle, turning it over and over, wondering if you could OD on it, start sprouting leaves on your shoulders, tiny green vines curling around your ankles.

But what about the loft? The will was so typical of her mother. She had always loved to move people around like chess pieces. Charlotte got out the Sunday paper and tried to figure out what it was really worth.

First she read the giant ad from Corcoran Realty, featuring a picture of a very groomed blond woman. Here was one loft selling for two million four hundred thousand dollars. The description read:

> Spectacular 2,250 sq ft duplex loft, very open and airy with 12' ceilings, original wood columns and beams, brick walls, large open kitchen, 1.5 bathrooms, wall of windows facing east into a 450 sq ft private Zen garden, all in excellent condition.

Well, there wasn't any Zen garden in her mother's loft, and she had no idea of the square footage, but there was certainly a large open kitchen, some annoying beams and at least twelve-foot ceilings and plenty of windows. Plus, there was that celebrity factor. Maybe someone would want to live where Corinne had lived and worked, thinking that gave it extra cachet.

She saw another ad for a loft just a couple of blocks away from Corinne's, described as "raw space." Well, Corinne's wasn't renovated, but it wasn't raw. Averaging the two ads, Charlotte figured she could probably get at least two million dollars, if not more, although she'd have to split it with William LaViolette. That would be about five hundred thousand dollars each after taxes. What would she do with five hundred thousand dollars? She could move to England, go to homeopathy school and live on the interest. She pictured herself growing old in a little bed-sit, drinking tea and wearing tweedy clothes.

But she didn't want to live in the loft. She didn't want to live with this William. She didn't want her life to change.

Charlotte sat down at her computer and started playing her favorite computer game, Covington. Paul had introduced her to it via an e-mail attachment soon after she'd started her job. Paul started out as the expert player, but slowly and surely Charlotte was getting better. She lost track of time when she played. The game involved day-to-day life in a British village that had been invaded by the underworld. The object of the game was to find the evil creatures and eradicate them.

Charlotte's character was a huntress named Varlata. She hunted out evil in all of its hiding places and lairs, in the darkest dungeons and the deepest woods. She hunted dragons, evil wizards, necromancers and the endless minions of Satan.

There was so much religious symbolism in Covington that at first it had made Charlotte, a born and bred atheist, uncomfortable.

Where was the atheist heroine, the secular villain, the agnostic action game? After a while, though, it had become comforting to have these strict delineations between good and evil, to know who the bad guys were and be able to hunt the monsters down in all of their many disguises. She stabbed the evil creatures with a jab of her magic dagger or a hail of arrows from her crossbow and they would vanish in a satisfying puff of noxious black smoke.

Charlotte had never realized she was so bloodthirsty until she played the game. There were less gory ways to kill the creatures, with magic or spells, but she enjoyed the hand-to-hand combat most.

Charlotte had died many times in Covington, forgetting to defend herself or to hit the escape key when she was surrounded. In Covington, however, death was never final. If you were killed, you would eventually resurface in town and could reanimate, for a small price.

Charlotte ran deep into the woods, seeking out mindless carnage. She slayed gorgons and wildebeests, hunted evil trolls who spewed fire and killed tiny imps whose fingertips leaked poison.

She was looking for the unicorn, who lived hidden deep in the forest, protected by a great blue dragon. There were rumors that the dragon had been injured, and its life force was being drained away by a powerful monster, Gorgona.

Charlotte usually didn't like to go this far into the forest without her companion, Ix (Paul). If she got killed in the wrong place, it could take her weeks to find her body and weapons and reanimate. Today, though, she didn't care. She searched and searched, finally hearing hints of the unicorn's movements, seeing the white glowing strands of mane that possessed magical healing powers. She gathered them up in her knapsack and kept going until her wrist ached from killing and her eyes were blurry from the dark screen.

Later, lying on her bed unable to sleep, she thought about unicorns and virgins and tried to remember the legends she had read about as a girl. When she was eleven, she had loved unicorns, had even torn out a page of the Unicorn Tapestries from an art book of her mother's. Her mother had been furious and then, after a few drinks, amused.

"Darling, unicorns are classic Freudian images—safe phallic symbols for little girls. That's all they are. They're not real," her mother had teased her. Charlotte had had no idea what she was talking about, she only knew she thought the unicorn was beautiful, with its snowy white coat, its gentle eyes. She wouldn't let them hurt it.

Charlotte got up and paced around the apartment. She turned on the television and watched an incomprehensible animated film on the Independent Film Channel until she felt tired enough to attempt sleep again.

And then, in the bathroom, brushing her teeth, she saw it, one of those horrible water bugs, crawling around boldly in her clean white bathtub. Usually only a few little ones appeared on summer nights when it was really humid, but she still dreaded them. She had a phobia about bugs. Imagined them falling in droves from the ceiling, taking over.

Charlotte closed her eyes as she quickly smashed it with the soap dish, breaking the ceramic dish until pieces of blue were scattered all over her bathtub. She cleaned up the mess, flushing the water bug down the toilet, and then made two extensive tours of the apartment to make sure there weren't any more lurking monsters. She sprayed Raid all around the bathroom, holding her breath, left the light by her bed on and eventually fell into fitful sleep.

*For trauma and shock, whether experienced recently
or in the past, try Star of Bethlehem.*

Chapter Four

S CHARLOTTE LEFT WORK, it was raining endlessly, the kind of summer rain that didn't seem to cool anything off. It was still raining when Charlotte entered her apartment, and inside she heard the drip from the skylight in her hallway, the slow drip, drip, drip that can drive a person insane. It reminded her of weekends when the twins used to beg her to play Chinese water torture with them. The victim, usually Charlotte, would be pinned down on the floor on a towel and the remaining two would slowly drip water on her forehead. The twins always begged to be the torturers. Charlotte hated equally being the victim or the torturer, but played just to please them.

Charlotte grabbed a bucket and put it under the drip. She called Mrs. Constantinople and told her about the leak.

"I know, I know," said Mrs. C in her I'm-not-going-to-fix-it voice. "Every year the same thing. The guy needs to fix the roof. I have to call my cousin Stavros. Monday I gonna call. So honey, you need a bucket. I come up?"

"No, it's okay. I have one."

"How's your father?"

Charlotte had finally told Mrs. C about her mother's death and her father's unexpected appearance. She instantly regretted telling Mrs. C about her father. Now, every time she ran into Mrs. C, all she could talk about was Charlotte's father, and Charlotte didn't have the heart to tell her that she hadn't seen him since the reading of the will.

"He's fine."

She watched television until late at night, listening to the harsh Chinese water torture drip into the bucket. She knew TV was a bad habit, but the rain made her nervous. She watched aimlessly, flicking between old episodes of *The Mary Tyler Moore Show* and infomercials about skin products. Whenever she watched infomercials, Charlotte always had an impulse to buy the one miraculous product that could change her life. Tonight, they were selling an eyebrow perfection system from Australia, a kit containing strips of molten wax that could remove unwanted hair and painlessly shape your eyebrows into elegant arches. Charlotte had never plucked her eyebrows, which were thick but neat, but the woman on the TV made it seem so easy, she was almost tempted to buy the product.

At midnight, Charlotte made her nightly cup of herbal tea. She alternated between chamomile and a special calming mixture she made herself, comprised of hawthorn berries, lime flowers and skullcap.

In the middle of a dream about David Duchovny, the way he used to look in *The X-Files,* she woke up. It was a long languid dream in which he was lying behind her, nuzzling into her neck. Charlotte was suffused with a warm glow when suddenly she felt something on her. She opened her eyes and saw something dark scurrying across her bedspread.

"Oh my god. Oh my god!" Charlotte jumped out of the bed and into her shoes, flipping on all the light switches, the lamps and the ugly overhead fluorescents. Then she saw it, a huge black water bug, poised on the edge of her bed like an evil omen.

"Stay right there," she ordered it. Charlotte grabbed the can of Raid she kept under the kitchen sink and threw on a T-shirt. She felt clammy and dirty, as if it were crawling on her.

When she got back into her bedroom, she didn't see the bug and she felt a rush of sheer terror. She kept brushing off her T-shirt and her legs and arms. She put on a pair of her sturdiest shoes, hiking boots that would be good for crushing.

Cautiously, she edged over to the bed and gave the bedspread a good shake. The evil bug scurried out and she doused it with Raid. She kept spraying and spraying and spraying, the way people shoot people in movies, over and over again, emptying their guns, way after the targets are dead, the way she killed monsters in Covington. The bug was sturdier than any monster, though, still moving purposefully after she had emptied half a can of Raid onto its dark hard shell. The room reeked of Raid, and she put a dishtowel over her mouth to block the sickly-smelling fumes, which probably caused some incurable disease.

And then, just when she thought she had killed it, that she was safe, she advanced toward the creature, sliding her hiking boots across the floor, until it suddenly came to life like one of the undead and she had to start spraying all over again.

Finally, it moved slower and slower, until it stopped moving at all and died, all six legs upturned on the carpet.

And then there was the problem of disposal. She couldn't pick it up. Even though it was dead, it was still terrifying and disgusting. It was three in the morning, so she didn't feel right turning on the vacuum cleaner. Finally, she got out the broom and dustpan and gingerly swept it into a Bloomie's bag and dumped it in the trash.

But she kept seeing it. That huge black creature of doom. What am I going to do? she thought. What am I going to do?

Luckily, when she was growing up, there had been few bugs in the loft. Her mother always had some mangy cat hanging around that took care of them.

That's it. I'll get a cat. But then she remembered Mrs. C's prohibitions against cats and children in her apartment. She would have neither of them in the place. "They ruin it," she would mutter, "especially children."

Charlotte walked back into the bedroom, throwing open the windows to air out the smell. Then she looked up at her light blue polyester curtains and saw another black shape moving quickly along the top of the windowsill. She tried to spray it, but it darted out of reach, out of sight behind the curtain.

Charlotte got completely dressed in heavy clothes, despite the heat. Sleep was out of the question. For the first time since her mother's death, she longed for Corinne to appear in person to dismiss her fears, call her an idiot, ask her what the hell she was doing living in the back of the beyond anyway, tell her she was being such a baby about a few little bugs. If she had seen the bugs Corinne had seen, well, *those* were bugs.

Corinne was gone, but she could go over to the loft if she wanted. She could even stay there for a few days. She had the keys. She had the right.

Charlotte packed up her clothes for the next day, her laptop, her alarm clock and some of her herbal remedies. Her hands were shaking. She called the car service. Grabbed the keys. Waited outside for the car. It was four in the morning and she was on her way back.

After a short cab ride across the Queensboro Bridge and down Broadway, she pushed open the heavy door to the loft, flicking on the light switch. Luckily, everything was still on: electricity, phone, cable. The loft seemed huge and empty without the familiar sculptures blocking all the passageways. The Guggenheim was storing the work Corinne had donated.

Charlotte walked around. The loft was almost completely open except for two bedrooms with makeshift doors, a bathroom and a huge open space that was living room, kitchen and studio all in one. At different points in history and with boyfriends and husbands of varying construction ability, rooms had been made and unmade, rooms with plastic walls, rooms separated by Japanese screens. Splintery plywood had been dragged up the four interminable flights of stairs when the elevator wasn't working.

Charlotte went into her mother's room and lay down under the soft Egyptian cotton sheets of her bed, but she couldn't sleep. She still felt like things were crawling on her. She went in the bathroom and washed her face with the hottest water she could stand, drying her face on her mother's purple Chinese bathrobe.

She took the bathrobe out of the bathroom and folded it neatly. What was she going to do with her mother's things? Maybe she could give them away somewhere. Maybe some art student would create an installation out of all her things. Or maybe she should just give them to Goodwill.

Charlotte got up and started to pull everything out of the closets, out of suitcases, out of old hat boxes. She got out some large green garbage bags and started sorting everything into piles, piles of velvet, piles of embroidered jackets, scarves, hats, sweaters, shawls. It seemed very important that her mother's things be organized. Some of the fabrics, antiques to begin with, were thick, lush and starting to fall to pieces. The clothes brought back memories of playing dress-up by herself, sinking into piles of exotic outfits, becoming a sheikh or dancing girl with a wrap of faded silk.

Charlotte picked up a long scarf with tattered fringes. Wrapped it around her neck. Put on a red wool cardigan. The wool was itchy and in places moths had eaten through it. She took them off and folded each item carefully. She folded velvet curtains, dust rising in waves like mist. She sneezed uncontrollably. She was allergic to dust, mold, and pollen, but she refused to get allergy shots. She treated herself with ephedra (in moderation) and mullein and homeopathic remedies. Charlotte folded scarves, sweaters and shawls. Shawls had come back in style. Charlotte saw business-women tossing shawls over their shoulders on their way to their jobs as corporate executives. But for Corinne, shawls had never gone out of style. She always wore the same things: shawls and berets and zip-up black leather or suede boots with Louis heels. She had unkempt frizzy brown hair and short bitten-off nails, but people looked up when she entered a room to see who she was. The women Charlotte saw on her way to work placed their shawls carefully around their bony shoulders according to the current wisdom of *Elle* and *Vogue,* but Charlotte's mother used to drape herself as if she were the work of art.

Charlotte, on the other hand, always dressed to appear incon-spicuous. She hated the idea that anyone was staring at her.

She got up to wash her hands.

❦

How could it be that two weeks after her mother died, the apart-ment still smelled like her? The smell was a combination of

Shalimar, acrylic paint and those awful cigarettes she used to smoke.

Lung cancer was what she should have died of, the way she used to smoke those things. A long painful death from lung cancer, coughing and complaining and making everyone around her miserable for years.

Charlotte hunted around for a cigarette, her fingers sliding along the dusty mantels and flat surfaces, her mother's usual hiding places. She found a pack in a tin breadbasket in the kitchen with a few still left in it. Balkan Sobranies. They smelled stale and delicious. She found her purse and took out matches from a restaurant called Frites she had gone to with the twins. She always took matches even though she didn't smoke. She lit a Sobranie and inhaled deeply. She didn't cough. She waved her tattered fringe and slowly smoked the cigarette.

Walking around, Charlotte found a heavy clinking bag on the dresser and emptied it onto the floor. Jewelry poured out, the heavy earth goddess jewelry her mother preferred. Corinne loved warm oddly shaped stones, chunks of turquoise, amber or fire opal. She despised diamonds, calling them "overpriced ice chips for people who don't know any better." She loved stones with texture—it could be a giant piece of beach glass, but if it caught the light correctly, Corinne would wear it to an opening and people would admire it, thinking it a precious stone they hadn't seen before.

Charlotte had also had a special outfit for openings. She used to wear it any time her mother would let her. It was a black velvet dress with lace at the sleeves. In it she felt like Sara Crewe, before Sara's father became sick with brain fever in India and she was sent off to the attic. She wanted to wear that dress long past the time the sleeves shrank above her growing wrists and the dress became a micro-mini. "You look like a little ghoul," Corinne used to say.

Well, you did.

You are not real.

Reality is vastly overrated. Hey, Charlotte, I've got an idea—why don't you give all that to the Met? I'm sure they'll grab it up.

Corinne had always had a thing about the Metropolitan Museum because they had never acknowledged her, never bought any of her pieces. Even though the Met rarely showed her type of art, except for some special exhibit, she felt slighted that they never approached her. MoMA had bought a few drawings, the Whitney had a sculpture and the Guggenheim was in love with her, but the Met was what she had always wanted.

I'll suggest that to Tanya—about the clothes. Hey, Corinne, what does it feel like? Not being alive?

Silence.

In the morning, Charlotte stood in front of the huge gold mirror that her mother had always posed in front of when she was getting dressed. They had found the mirror at a flea market and had spray-painted it antique gold. Charlotte didn't have a full-length mirror in her apartment, so it was a shock to see herself from head to toe. Next to her mother's richly colored clothes and the red walls of the bedroom, Charlotte looked dowdy. Her pants were good quality, pleated, beige.

A blouse and slacks, Charlotte, isn't that just a little bit boring?

Charlotte took a dress out of the closet, from among the summer clothes of her mother's she hadn't packed away yet. It was a simple dress she had only seen her mother wear a couple of times, probably because it was a little small for her, but it was a beautiful deep scarlet red. Charlotte kicked off her shoes, stepped out of her pants and put it on. It fit her perfectly.

Not bad, and for the record, it wasn't too small, I just didn't like it. But Charlotte, you've got to do something about that hair!

Maybe you're right.

～

Charlotte went outside, blinking in the bright sunlight. She had only gotten four hours' sleep and she wandered along West Broadway in a daze. So many of the places she remembered as a child were gone, used clothing stores and corner delis replaced by glittering makeup stores and upscale boutiques.

Charlotte stood outside the door of a hair salon. It was silver and chrome, like a starship. She walked in the door slowly, agreed to a haircut and was whisked to a dressing cubicle to take off her sundress and put on a wraparound robe. Feeling naked, she clutched the robe tightly around her body and sat waiting. Beautiful people kept walking by, people with their hair crisscrossed with aluminum foil, women with long blond manes and men in tight leather pants. Charlotte felt drab and insignificant.

Finally, a stocky Asian woman with a T-shirt that said SUPER-STAR came up to her, talking fast. "Hi, I'm Blade, your stylist. That's not my real name, we all have to have stage names here. There's Velvet and Pepper over there. It's fun, kind of like that game you play where you find your stripper name. You take the name of your pet as a child and then your middle name. Like, my dog was named Brandy and my middle name is Diane, so I'd be Brandy Diane."

"I don't have a middle name," Charlotte admitted.

"Okay, what's your pet's name?"

"Well, we had a cat named Vronsky and one named Roark."

"I'm not sure you're stripper material."

Blade's assistant brought Charlotte a cappuccino and Blade gave her a scalp massage. The touch of Blade's hands on her head made her feel like crying, but Charlotte scrunched her eyes together, gritted her teeth and forced herself not to think of her mother's clothes without her mother in them.

"Are you okay?" asked Blade. "Don't be nervous. Just relax, honey, leave the haircut to me."

Charlotte closed her eyes. She thought of acting class. Next week they were going to do a new exercise in which they were going to learn how to be vulnerable in front of an audience. She wondered if that guy would be there, the one who had saved her from being crushed by *War and Peace*. She pictured herself doing a love scene with him and the class clapping at how authentic they were.

"So, what do you think?

Charlotte started and looked down at the clumps of hair around her. Then she looked at her new self in the mirror.

Her hair was short. Just below her ears. She had spiky bangs in the front, and in the back her hair fit her head like a sleek cap.

Blade was rubbing a substance called Fixolater into her hair. "This will make it stand up a little bit. I know it's a shock, but you'll get used to it. It shows off your neck."

Charlotte was speechless. She put her hand up to the back of her neck. It was shorn like a sheep.

Blade twirled her around and Charlotte saw the nape of her neck for the first time in memory. It looked so naked.

"Are you okay?"

"I guess."

"You hate it, don't you? I knew it," said Blade, sounding insecure.

"No, I like it, really." Charlotte paid the bill in a daze, putting a twenty in a tiny envelope for Blade.

As Charlotte walked out of the salon, several people said, "Nice cut."

Exhausted and disoriented, she finally arrived back at the loft. All she wanted to do was sink into her mother's bed and absorb the change she had made. But when she opened the door, her so-called father was sprawled out on the floor, a glass of red wine in his hand, looking at the piles of jewelry on the floor.

For those who find their lives unhappy and withdraw
into fantasy worlds, we recommend Clematis.

Chapter Five

C HARLOTTE LEANED ON the heavy steel door of her mother's loft and stared at him. Seeing that man, her so-called father, lounging around like he belonged there, fingering her mother's jewelry, she was speechless. As she stood there staring at him, William got to his feet, a chunky turquoise bracelet still dangling from his fingers. "Charlotte, I'm so glad you're here."

"What are you doing here?" Charlotte asked, leaning up against the doorframe, feeling as if she were the intruder. She became conscious of the tiny hairs from her haircut bristling against her bare neck.

William stood up, his knees cracking. He handed her the bracelet and she took it, slipping it onto her wrist without thinking. She remembered that her mother had bought the bracelet during a trip to Mexico. For several months afterward, she had painted strange self-portraits pierced with tiny arrows, in the style of Frieda Kahlo, drinking margaritas nonstop.

"Charlotte, I'm really sorry to startle you, but I thought you knew I was coming. I called your apartment and left messages. Several times. And Mr. Sneed gave me the keys."

Since her mother's death, it was true that ordinary tasks like listening to the answering machine had seemed irrelevant. But still, this wasn't right.

Charlotte knelt down and started picking up the jewelry and putting it on the kitchen counter. She sorted it into piles. Bracelets, necklaces, rings.

"This is my mother's jewelry," she said. Her voice sounded strange and loud. "I don't know if you remember, but she loved to wear jewelry. It's funny, I can't wear any jewelry. Necklaces make me feel like I'm choking, rings give me a rash. I don't even have my ears pierced. I don't know why I'm telling you this. I don't know why you're here. Don't you have a place to live of your own?"

"Charlotte, I really think this could work out—for both of us. Can't we talk about it?"

"What's there to talk about?" She felt enveloped in anger, like a force field.

"Your mother wanted us to live here, together. She must have had a good reason."

"You could be a mass murderer, for all I know."

He laughed.

"It's not funny."

"I know. But I'm not a mass murderer."

Charlotte stopped sorting the jewelry and looked at him. "Do you think if you were, you'd admit it?"

It was true, he looked harmless enough. He was wearing a white T-shirt that said JOHNNY CASH and worn blue jeans. She imagined telling him to get out and leave her alone. But then what would happen? Legally, they both had to live here for a full year, or the loft would be sold and the proceeds given to charity. But if she could last through a year with him, they could sell it and keep the money. With her share of the money she could buy her own place. Upstate. Someplace with a garden to grow herbs.

"You look different."

Charlotte touched her hair with her fingers. "I had my hair cut." She walked over to the radio and turned it off.

"I take it you don't like country music."

"I hate it," she said vehemently, although it wasn't really true. Even if he was going to live here, he didn't have to know her.

She started walking into the main room, where all there was left of her mother was a gold velvet couch, a coffee table and a couple of ratty brown corduroy chairs. He followed her, looking at the radio.

"Classical?"

"It's okay."

"I guess jazz is out of the question."

"Detest it."

"Charlotte, if I had known, I would have—"

"A lot of people don't like jazz, it's no big deal."

"I mean about you."

"It doesn't matter. You didn't know. It's the past." Charlotte didn't want to hear him talk about how he would have been a great father if he had known about her existence. He should have known. Parents are supposed to just know. How could he not have known?

"I tried to call your mother, after we split up, but she didn't want anything to do with me."

Charlotte walked back into the kitchen and filled up the kettle to make tea, a reflex action. She looked through the cabinets, but her mother only had one exotic-looking canister from Fortnum and Mason. She opened it hopefully, but there were only a few dusty tea leaves left clinging to the sides of the empty jar.

Charlotte saw William's suitcases lined up neatly against a wall. There weren't many: one battered old square suitcase, a garment bag, a guitar case and a wrapped-up package that looked like an easel. Looking at the bags, their living here together seemed like an accomplished fact, something she couldn't fight. Even if she didn't stay, she could see he would. She felt like a landlady in an old movie, dealing with an unwelcome tenant.

"Okay, I guess. You can have the room at the end of the hall. The green one. I'll stay in the main bedroom. We'll stay out of each other's way. Okay?"

"Charlotte."

She ignored him, shutting the door to her mother's room, falling into the bed as if she had taken a sleeping potion.

❦

Charlotte woke up a few hours later in her mother's red dress, lying on a dusty quilt. She sneezed and glanced over at the mirror. Her hair was short, her mother was gone and there was something important she had to do. Acting class. She opened the door to her room slowly, but she didn't hear anyone. Maybe he went out. This was horrible, having to creep around the loft avoiding him.

In the bathroom she washed her face. Her hair was sticking up and she wet it down with water. She didn't have time to take a shower or change, or she would be late.

❦

Charlotte hurried toward her acting class. It was a warm clear night. The buildings were lit up in the distance and for a moment Charlotte thought about gravity, trying to imagine the planet spinning, how everything was glued down with an invisible force. But what if the gravity started failing and things started drifting off?

Her mother had died. Anything could happen. Charlotte felt her heart beat hard inside her chest.

Charlotte snuck into the back of the class. They were already in the midst of doing an exercise in which each person had to go up onstage and the class had to describe him or her with adjectives. A guy named Steve was onstage now, and they were shouting out adjectives to him: *Strong. Reliable. Athletic.* The person onstage had to repeat the words back to the class. Steve repeated them back. The teacher, Susan, stood up and said, "Own the words. Be the words."

Steve yelled out, *Strong. Reliable.* Made a muscle with his arm and said, *Athletic.*

When Jodee got up onstage, she gave the audience her best sex-kitten look. As if on cue, a guy yelled out, *Sexy.* She pranced around the stage repeating back the words in an exaggerated fashion: *Cute. Sexy. Petite.* A woman yelled out *Aggressive* and Jodee gave her a dirty look.

"Say it," said Susan. "And stay still; moving is a way of deflecting emotion."

Aggressive, said Jodee sullenly, standing like a statue.

"Good job, Jodee," said Susan, as she walked back.

Someone else yelled *Actress* and everyone laughed.

"*Actress* is not a character trait," said Susan, smiling, and then it was Charlotte's turn.

She felt glued to her chair but forced herself to get up with simple commands. Feet down. Feet forward. Up the stairs. On the stage.

The journey up to the stage was endless and when she finally arrived on the small wooden platform, it felt strange to be the one up there, looking out at everyone. She stood paralyzed as the class said, *Quiet. Shy. Kind.* She repeated, *Quiet. Shy. Kind.*

"Louder," yelled Susan.

Quiet. Shy. Kind.

She was disappointed with her descriptor words. Would this librarian stereotype follow her around forever? Librarians were seen as quiet, sensible, nerdy, inhibited. She didn't want to be inhibited. She didn't even think she was like that deep down. It just seemed easier sometimes to observe people than be observed. She stood on the stage, trying not to be like that. She imagined herself as Varlata, tough and sexy. How long was she going to have to stand up there anyway?

Charlotte saw Colin, the Irish guy, and he said, *Intriguing.* She repeated, *Intriguing.* She was grateful to him for giving her a good adjective and gave it an extra effort, repeating the word with more feeling. *Intriguing,* she said, trying to be.

When she got back to the loft, it was dark and empty. Although she didn't want William here, she felt annoyed in spite of herself. Where was he? Did he just think he could come and go as he pleased?

*Holly is the flower remedy for feelings
of suspicion and anger.*

Chapter Six

CHARLOTTE WOKE UP to the sounds of birds on her nature alarm clock. The birds were only one out of the five available nature sounds, but waterfall, rain, mist and brook all sounded like static to Charlotte. She pressed the snooze button, then opened her eyes, slowly becoming aware of her surroundings. It was hot, paint was peeling off the walls and garbage trucks were racing their engines outside the flimsy windows. In fact, the whole loft was shaking as if the building was in an earthquake. Everything was familiar, but one thing was missing.

Charlotte sat up in bed and sneezed four times in rapid succession. She made a mental note to buy a vacuum cleaner with a HEPA filter and get allergen barriers for all the pillows. She strained to hear signs of William, but all was quiet.

Charlotte put on her bathrobe and her slippers and walked out into the hall, trying to be as quiet as possible. She padded into the kitchen and started making coffee. Except now it was no longer just coffee. It was, Should I make enough coffee for that strange man who is living here with me in my mother's loft? Her mother had left no food in the loft, so Charlotte had stocked up on French Guatemalan coffee, vegetarian frozen dinners and fresh fruit. She liked shopping in Soho, although everything cost twice as much as anywhere else. They had organic food here, something people in Astoria would scoff at. Once, she went to a party at her landlady's for her son (the good son), and she had tried to refuse an eight-foot hero sandwich with twelve kinds of Italian meat on it.

"Eat something," they had said, pressing an enormous slab of sandwich at her.

"She's too skinny."

"Actually," Charlotte had confessed unwillingly, "I don't eat meat."

They had looked at Charlotte as if she were the Antichrist.

⁂

Charlotte ended up making enough coffee for William too, wondering if he was the type to sleep all day. Maybe they would never see each other. They would just go through their days on totally opposite schedules. That would probably be for the best. Charlotte drank her coffee quickly, took an abbreviated shower and got dressed, all the while waiting for movement down the hall.

Finally, as she was getting ready to leave, she heard stirring in William's room. William came out, his eyes barely open. "Good morning."

"Morning," said Charlotte, looking at his T-shirt (today it said RY COODER, whoever he was) and wondering why he looked so much more at home here than she felt. He made a beeline for the coffee.

"There are cups over there in that blue cabinet." She pointed a finger.

"Thanks."

Charlotte sipped her coffee and watched William from a distance. She had wanted him to appear, but now that he was here, she wanted him to leave. She wanted something from him, but when he was there, she just felt angry and powerless.

"So, Charlotte, when's your birthday?"

"Why, you want to send me thirty-three cards?"

William smiled like she had been trying to be funny. "No, I was just curious."

"July twentieth."

"A Cancer, huh?"

"I guess."

"I'm a Sagittarius, not that I'm really into all that."

"Congratulations." Charlotte picked up her handbag. "Make sure you double lock the door when you leave."

"Okay. I'll see you later, Charlotte."

❦

It was a relief to get to her desk, turn on the computer and hear its tinny electric voice saying good morning. It was amazing how comforting an electronic voice could be.

She checked the messages and started working on a project researching experimental drugs for degenerative diseases. Charlotte had thought a lot about ways to die and decided that a degenerative disease must be one of the worst ways, your abilities draining away bit by bit, until you couldn't do anything for yourself.

Charlotte had always had a vision of taking care of her mother in her old age, weaning her off wine and vodka with herbal concoctions, getting really close like mothers and daughters in Lifetime Channel movies. Of course, it never would have happened. Her mother would have found some impressionable art student to take care of her. Someone to hear all her stories for the first time, to bring her drinks and never mention AA. Corinne believed that the consumption of alcohol was fundamental to her production of art and that inspiration flowed through her much more effectively from a bottle of French wine.

"Do you think Picasso went to a twelve-step meeting?" she would scream at Charlotte if she dared suggest her mother needed to stop drinking. "Do you think Rodin spilled his guts to pathetic strangers? No, they painted, they sculpted, they created. Anyway, alcohol doesn't affect me the way it does your average person."

Charlotte continued her research. It angered her how little the drug companies and doctors really knew about any of these diseases. Many of the drugs had so many side effects that if you took them long enough you could develop another disease, possibly worse than the one you originally had. That's what she liked about homeopathy, its subtle mysterious action, its philosophy of lack of harm.

Paul called. "How are you holding up, Charlotte?"

"I'm fine. Did I tell you my father is actually living with me in the loft now?"

"You're kidding."

"Unfortunately, I'm not. I know, it seems like the perfect plot for a soap opera—dead father suddenly appears after thirty-three years."

"What's he like?"

"I don't know and I'm not sure I want to."

"How long is he going to stay?"

"A year—and then we move out and never have to see each

other again. We can sell the loft, split the money and go our separate ways."

"If you can make it that long. Well, keep me updated."

Charlotte forced herself to go back to Queens to get her stuff. She was going to bring just the essentials with her, put the rest in storage. Getting off the subway, she didn't feel the same sense of comfort she usually did. The stores seemed archaic, dirty, the people dowdy. Living in Soho for a few days, her perspective had already changed. Looking around, it was as if Astoria were trapped in a time warp. The women looked unhealthy, unhappy, burdened by chores. The men spent their free time in what they called men's clubs, nondescript little rooms where they smoked and played cards and avoided their families.

She went to Key Food for a few things to take back with her. As she was picking up some Smart Puffs in the snack aisle, she saw the woman with no front teeth who lived in a house on her block. The woman had silvery white hair and a vicious dog. First she was in the frozen food aisle. Then the cereal aisle. Everywhere Charlotte went, the woman was right in front of her, glaring at Charlotte as if she hated her. She's just self-conscious because of her teeth, Charlotte told herself, but the woman was beginning to remind her of a witch. In fact, the whole supermarket was beginning to seem Felliniesque. She went over to the TEN ITEMS OR LESS line, where a couple had made a towering pile of every kind of meat imaginable—kielbasa, hot dogs, flank steak and pigs' feet—which they were playing with, tossing hot dogs up in the air and then grinning. She skipped that aisle and stood in front of an old man who was slowly snipping away at a plastic bag with a small pair of nail scissors in front of a cart full of flan. Charlotte finally dropped her Smart Puffs and herbal tea in the magazine rack and left, empty-handed and anxious, as a homeless woman in the alleyway counted her refundable cans and applied lipstick in a wide arc all around her mouth.

Charlotte ran into her landlady on the stoop. Mrs. C started talking as if she and Charlotte had been in the midst of a conversation.

"If I had it all to do over again, I wouldn't do any of it—husband, kids, house. I'm telling you the truth, Charlotte, I wouldn't do it."

She told Charlotte that there had been another leak in her apartment, and they went up to look at it. There was a bucket in the living room, and the ugly speckled green carpet was soaked. Charlotte felt so relieved that she wasn't living there.

"I can't deal with this anymore," said Mrs. C. "I'm not happy. I came from Greece thirty years ago, and now all I do is babysit and work and worry about this house."

Charlotte didn't know what to say. She wanted to tell Mrs. C to sell everything, leave her husband and run away, but she knew that wasn't going to happen.

Charlotte and Mrs. C cleaned up the rest of the mess and Charlotte suggested they should go out to one of the local Greek cafés.

Mrs. C agreed reluctantly. "I never come in here," she said, walking in the door of the café hesitantly, as if they were entering a house of ill repute. She nodded sternly at some men she knew and Charlotte ordered some cookies and two frappés. Mrs. C complained about the service, the price, the quality of the cookies and the sweetness of the frappés, but Charlotte could tell she was having a good time.

"I need to tell you something," said Charlotte.

"Oh my god, it's not the cancer, is it?"

"No, I'm fine."

"Thank God!"

"It's about the apartment."

"I'm gonna fix that leak, I swear to you."

"No, it's not that. I've decided to move in with my father."

Mrs. C crumpled as if she had been hit in stomach. "Charlotte, you're breaking my heart here. You're the best tenant I ever had. Why do you have to leave?"

"Mrs. C, I need to do this."

"What if I fix the place up?"

"No, I've made up my mind, but it wouldn't be a bad idea to renovate—paint, maybe put down some new tiles. I'm sure you could get a lot more money for the place."

Mrs. C perked up. "How much?"

"I don't know, you could probably charge fifteen hundred if you fixed it up."

"How'm I gonna afford to fix it up?" said Mrs. C, staring into the depths of her frappé, but Charlotte could tell the wheels of finance were already turning in her mind. "Fifteen hundred dollars, you really think so?"

"I do."

❧

When they went back to the apartment, Charlotte packed up what she considered essential—some clothes, more remedies, some books and papers and a few other items—and then called the car service.

Mrs. C came out and wished her good luck.

"I'll pay you till the end of next month," said Charlotte.

"You're a good girl," said Mrs. C, patting her on the shoulder. "Men, they're worthless."

When the car service came, Mrs. C helped Charlotte with her bags and told her to be careful.

"They rob you blind in the city, watch out." She said something in Greek to the driver and then gave Charlotte a hug.

Charlotte wondered if anything would ever get better for Mrs. C. She hoped so, but the odds seemed unlikely. She should kick out all those useless men and start having some fun. As they drove onto the Queensboro Bridge, Charlotte gave it a long last look. She always thought the Queensboro Bridge was the most beautiful bridge of all, with its gothic spires and intricate web of metal, like the entrance to some otherworldly castle. Now she was leaving the castle, venturing into foreign lands. Queens had been a kind of safe harbor for her, a hideout, where no one knew her and she could exist in her own little cocoon.

*For those whose self-reliance can make them seem
too proud and disdainful of others,
Water Violet can help them connect with others.*

Chapter Seven

I N ACTING CLASS, Charlotte was learning about *not* acting.
Not acting was one of the most important tenets of the studio. Acting was artificial. Not acting was about finding the
truth of your character—and eventually yourself.

Instead of acting, you were supposed to channel emotional
events that had happened to you directly into the character. If you
really experience an emotion, the audience will believe you. At
The Craft, they learned how to do this with sense-memory exercises. The object was to feel how things had felt to you at the
time—the tastes, the sights, even the smells—and store it away, to
pull out the memory as needed.

Charlotte had spent so much time as a child in her own imaginary world that this was not difficult for her. She used to play two
games, alternating between them. One was called Queen of the
Forest and the other Starvation. In Queen of the Forest, she com-
manded everything around her: all the trees, the grass, the wind and

the sun. They were all her loyal subjects, and they would do her bidding. She would command the sun to shine, the breeze to blow, and fairies to sound their tiny flower trumpets. And she would do all this from the strategic vantage point of one of the loft windowsills.

In Starvation, she was trapped on a desert island and had to make delicious meals out of nothing and forage for food à la Robinson Crusoe. She made meals out of pretend twigs and palm fronds, cooking them over an imaginary fire into delicious stews and casseroles. Sometimes she would bake actual chocolate chip cookies and imagine the chips were tiny tropical nuts she had collected on her beach.

Charlotte was totally engrossed in these games when she played. They became more real to her than her day-to-day life. When she explained the games to her mother, Corinne always laughed at her. Once, she told Charlotte that she had a vivid imagination, but she was not sure she was all there, pointing at Charlotte's head.

❦

Charlotte spotted Colin in the back of the room, taking notes. He was so good-looking it was hard not to stare at him. According to the grapevine, he got all his classes for free as a result of his arrangement with Susan. Jodee from ballet was also in her classes, and lately her clothing seemed to be undergoing a shrinkage process, as if someone were snipping away at them in her sleep, until her belly-button ring was fully exposed. Jodee had had a brief moment of fame, having appeared in a Clearasil commercial when she was fifteen, but her career had stalled ever since.

❦

The acting exercise of the day involved writing down a list of the top ten things they were afraid of.

Charlotte couldn't think of anything to write. She was afraid of too many things. Everyone around her was scribbling furiously, intent on his or her list.

Finally she wrote:

> *Top ten things I am afraid of:*
> 1. *Writing down what I'm afraid of*
> 2. *The dark*
> 3. *Bugs*
> 4. *Death*
> 5. *Getting trapped in a car underwater*
> 6. *Not being able to breathe*
> 7. *Never falling in love*
> 8. *Having to read this out loud*
> 9. *Being humiliated in front of the class.*

She got stuck on number 10. Luckily, they didn't have to read their own lists out loud. It was anonymous. Everyone crumpled up his or her bit of paper into a hat and they each picked one out to read.

A lot of people were afraid of getting up on a real stage, of forgetting their lines, of not succeeding, of not getting a break, of being alone. When one of the girls read Charlotte's list out loud, everyone laughed as if she had meant it to be funny. Charlotte thought she sounded like a crazy person, a phobic crazy person. She thought of a number 10: fear of being institutionalized for crippling emotional fears.

At the break, Jodee and Charlotte moseyed down to the local coffee bar, which resembled a run-down living room, furnished with messy overstuffed couches and spindly wooden coffee tables. Over her nonfat decaf cappuccino, Jodee told Charlotte her life story. She had divorced parents, both living in the city, who despised each other. She was an only child. She lived in an apartment paid for by her wealthy parents only a few blocks from both of them, on East End Avenue. They paid for acting school and voice lessons as well, but apart from that she was "totally on my own."

"My mom was a total stage mom. She was always putting me in those creepy beauty contests, like Jon Benet-Ramsey, when I was like five years old. How about yours?"

"Dead," said Charlotte, enjoying the shock value and the total silence for a moment as Jodee regrouped.

"Were you little?" asked Jodee, as if that would make it less shocking.

"No, it was a month ago."

"Oh my god, that's awful. You must be going through all these emotions. You could totally use that in your acting."

"I don't know—I don't think it's really sunk in yet."

"Were you close to your mom? I'd die if something happened to my mom."

"She traveled a lot."

"I know exactly what you mean. My father is constantly going to Italy for leather—he's in the garment business—and I'm lucky if he brings me back a lousy bottle of extra virgin. But I can't imagine . . . I'm really sorry about your mom." Jodee toyed with the foam on her cappuccino, relatively speechless.

"Thank you. So, when are we going to get our scene partners?" asked Charlotte, changing the subject.

"I don't know, maybe today. I hope I get Colin and a steamy love scene—he's way hot."

Charlotte remembered him leaning over in class the other day.

He smelled good too, like cigarettes and cologne and something spicy.

"What about your boyfriend, the one with the prostate problem?"

"Over. Finito. He was too old for me anyway."

When they got back to class, the postings for scene partners were written on the chalkboard outside the classroom. Everyone was milling around nervously, looking for their name.

Charlotte approached the tiny board slowly until the names gradually came into focus. She saw her name and then Colin's name in a row. Jodee was standing in back of her, reading over her shoulder. Charlotte traced their names with her finger. Charlotte Stiles. Colin Brody. *Summer and Smoke.* That must be the play they were going to be doing.

"No way. I can't believe you are going to be doing a scene with Colin. Unbelievable. I got stuck with Heather. It's not fair. I act much better with men."

Colin wasn't in class when they sat down inside. Everyone else had paired up and whipped out Palm Pilots and were busy planning rehearsals and arguing about whose neighborhood to meet in. Charlotte sat by herself and wondered what *Summer and Smoke* was about. Something about lung cancer, perhaps?

Susan came over to Charlotte, smiling. "It's a great role for you, and Colin will be perfect because you are just starting out."

She scribbled something on a piece of paper and handed it to Charlotte. "Here's his number so you can arrange a time to meet."

Susan explained that scene partners had to meet with each

other twice a week until the performance, and then put on the scene in front of the whole class. There were strict rules, which she made everyone write down:

> **Always meet at a neutral place.**
> **Maintain a professional distance.**
> **No alcohol, no drugs and no inappropriate behavior.**
> **Above all, never get intimately involved with a scene partner.**

When Charlotte left the class, she was still clutching the little piece of paper with the phone number. Her scene partner. Colin.

Back at the loft, Charlotte decided to go to Covington instead of calling Colin. She set up her laptop and logged on. Paul was on-line already in his personality of Ix the Mage.

After Paul had introduced Charlotte to the role-playing game she had quickly become addicted. Sometimes it was preferable to reality.

Today she just wanted to chat with Paul and maybe go into the woods and kill a dragon or look for the unicorn. It was funny, she would never pick up the phone to call him, but she would go on-line to see him.

Charlotte and Paul had acquired enough status in the game that they were no longer newbies, novice players likely to be killed as soon as they appeared or robbed by bands of marauding gypsies.

She went into the tavern and ordered a mead. She saw Ix at the far end of the bar. He hailed her and they clinked their virtual tankards.

"And how fares the guest at your home, your uncle I believe it is, home from parts afar?"

"My uncle and I are strangers," typed Charlotte, with a stamp of her virtual Roman sandal, "and so we shall remain."

"Yes," said Ix, "although he is family, Varlata."

"So he claims, Ix, so he claims."

They headed out together into the woods. After a few peaceful hours of hunting and slaying, Charlotte waved farewell to Ix and snapped her laptop closed as if she had been doing something shameful. For some reason, she didn't want William to see her playing the game.

The next morning, Charlotte woke up early, hearing vague clinking noises. She didn't think of herself as an angry person, but the sounds of that man in the apartment were grating on her nerves. She couldn't hear herself think through all the clanging in the kitchen. What was he doing anyway? She told herself to relax. To breathe. It wasn't her problem. She was calm. She was just going to pretend he didn't exist. Charlotte liked to do this with difficult problems and people. She knew it wasn't healthy, but sometimes it was just easier. Like when some crazy person sat down next to her on the subway, she would just say to herself *they don't exist, they don't exist.*

But he does exist, said her mother.

What do you want from me?

Just go out there and talk to him.

She ignored the voice and got ready to go out. Took a shower, wishing the bathroom door had a lock. He does not exist, she told herself, drying her hair, putting on her aromatherapy moisturizer, her sunblock, her homeopathic Traumeel cream for the nagging pain in her wrists she got after being on the computer too long.

When she was finished getting dressed, she walked cautiously out to the kitchen. William was chopping onions furiously.

"Charlotte, hi, how are you? Have you eaten?"

"Yes," said Charlotte, although it was untrue. She was actually starving.

"Oh, that's too bad, I was just making some eggs and I thought you might. . . ."

Charlotte tried to imagine a time when she had ever seen her mother cooking.

"I went shopping." William opened the refrigerator door with a flourish, showing her what he had bought. "I got eggs and cheese and cold cuts," he said proudly, taking out a waxed paper package labeled SALAMI.

"I'm a vegetarian."

"Oh," said William, putting the salami down on the counter. "For moral or health reasons?"

"I just don't eat meat, that's all."

"That's interesting. I once knew a girl who didn't eat meat. She wouldn't even wear leather shoes."

Charlotte glanced down at her flat black leather sandals, thinking that the last thing she wanted to hear was about some old girlfriend of his. She turned around and went back to her room. This was not going to work. She couldn't even look at him. He should have died, the way she had believed he had, and her mother should have lived.

She lay down on the bed, feeling angry and slightly guilty. Dialed Jules's number. Not home. This was ridiculous. She lived here. He was the intruder. If she wanted to eat something, she should just eat something. Charlotte walked back into the kitchen, trying to act nonchalant, took an Amy's organic burrito out of the freezer and stared at it, reading the ingredients: soy cheese, organic corn, black beans, expeller-pressed oil, whatever the hell expeller-pressed was.

"So, are you sure I can't tempt you with some eggs? I made an enormous amount. Do you eat eggs, or are you an ovo-lacto whatshamacallit?"

"I eat eggs," admitted Charlotte. The eggs did smell good, scrambled just right with scallions and some kind of soft cheese. "Okay, thanks," she said, taking a plate of eggs and sitting down in what passed for a dining room—a vast open space with a table made out of an old door and some mismatched chairs.

They sat eating the eggs quietly.

"What do you think?" asked William after a while.

"They're good."

"I mean about this situation."

Charlotte looked at him, trying to see herself in his face. The twins said he looked just like her, but she didn't see it. He wasn't ugly and he wasn't handsome, he was just some guy she would pass on the street and not give a second thought to, the kind of person who would come into her library and ask about antioxidants.

"I just can't believe Corinne wanted this. If she had wanted me to know who my father was, why wouldn't she have talked about it? She always said my father was dead."

"Dead, huh? I'm not surprised. How did I die?"

"Some rare disease. It was never specified."

"I hope I didn't suffer."

Charlotte smiled in spite of herself. "It's not funny."

"Corinne always thought she would die young," said William, clearing his throat.

"I know," said Charlotte. It was something that she always used to say. *Darlings, I'm not worried about the future, I'm not going to be here.*

"Do you think when you broke up, she knew?" Charlotte asked.

"About you?"

"Yes."

William stood up. "Honestly, Charlotte, I don't know. She could have gotten in touch with me if she wanted to."

"And what would you have done?"

He walked back and forth. "How does anyone know what he or she would have done thirty-three years ago? I do know that I'm glad you're here."

"I'm a little old to need a father."

"Well, I'm not used to being a father either, so maybe we can be friends."

"Maybe," said Charlotte with a shrug, picking up her plate and putting it in the sink. "Thanks for the eggs."

⁎

At the library, Charlotte worked steadily from nine to six, trying not to let thoughts or imaginary people like her mother intrude. Every once in a while, she would try to rehearse calling Colin, her new scene partner, but then lost her nerve before she actually made the call. She liked his name; it seemed exotic yet accessible.

She researched heart drugs. Apparently, scientists had discovered that heart cells could regenerate after a heart attack. There was also a theory that heart problems could be indicators of blocked emotions. Charlotte knew that willow and holly were good for emotional blockages. But what emotion had Corinne ever blocked? Fear, maybe. Loneliness, weakness.

Lately, since her mother's death, Charlotte sometimes thought she was going crazy. She would be walking down the street and the air would start to feel unsafe. She would try to imagine not being able to breathe, that feeling when you are swimming underwater, trying to go farther and farther, and your lungs feel like they are going to burst.

It was one thing to know, intellectually, that death was inevitable, but it was another to see that it happened in an instant, that someone you loved could disappear from the world in one phone call.

Charlotte fantasized that she had been the one who had died. What kind of funeral would there have been? Her mother would probably still have been the focus of attention, a figure straight out of Greek tragedy, wringing her hands and beating her breast.

Charlotte ate lunch outside, a tasteless veggie burger, some lentil salad and an apple. She tried to read her play, *Summer and Smoke,* but she couldn't focus on the words. It was a beautiful, sunny day and her mother was dead. The sun was too strong. The air felt unsafe. She tried to breathe in and out, concentrating on her diaphragm expanding and contracting, like they did in the relaxation exercises in acting class. The air is fine. It's just a simple anxiety attack, she told herself, but that didn't seem to help much.

In class, they had been told to spend some time learning more about their characters. Charlotte's assignment was to find an object that represented her character's emotional climate. She had gone to a florist and bought a delicate pink rose and pressed it between the pages of one of her old homeopathy books to dry. After a few days, the rose was frail and slightly curled up at the edges, just past its prime, like her character, Alma.

Even though she hadn't even met with Colin and started

rehearsing, Charlotte had bought a special Alma dress in a thrift store to wear for the performance. It was a faded floral print with tiny buttons down the front. The skirt was slightly full, ending midcalf. When Charlotte put it on, she began to feel very Alma-ish. Maybe it wasn't so much of a stretch. Charlotte wasn't a prude, but she wasn't exactly experienced either. In the play, Alma had only gone out with three men seriously, and Charlotte, in real life, had only gone out with two seriously, and slept with a grand total of three. And like Alma, there had been a desert between her and these men, especially in regard to sex. She had never enjoyed it much and she had never felt that *in love* feeling she thought she was supposed to feel. She read through the play, trying to get the feel of the character.

L'amour, l'amour, toujours l'amour.

Can you read my thoughts?

No, but I can read over your shoulder. You are nothing like that simpering Miss Alma.

Charlotte was flattered. She would have thought that her mother would see her just like Miss Alma: shy, repressed, alone. "Corinne, where are you?" she said aloud.

Silence.

It was just like when she was alive. Corinne would make some pronouncement and then proceed to the next thing, ignoring Charlotte entirely.

Gentian is the flower remedy for those who are easily discouraged.

Chapter Eight

*I*T HAD BEEN TWO months since Corinne's death. Jules and Charlotte were eating sandwiches inside the mausoleum where Corinne was interred. Some of the mausoleums at the cemetery were simply aboveground tombs, but Corinne's was a tiny little house you could actually enter, if you had the key.

"It's actually called a vestibule mausoleum," said Jules, reading from a brochure that she had picked up at the entrance to the cemetery. " 'Provides visitors with a secluded meditation area and a welcome retreat from inclement weather.' "

"I'm glad she's not underground."

Jules had brought a fuzzy pink blanket, so they picnicked on the cold stone floor, eating their lunch and drinking sparkling wine that Jules had brought in a cooler. Jules popped the cork and poured the wine into two paper cups.

"It's Italian. It's called prosecco."

"That's fitting. Corinne loved Italy, and her wine."

"Let's make a toast," said Jules. "Here's to Corinne, may she rest in peace and stop haunting her daughter, Charlotte."

They clinked their cups and sipped the wine.

Charlotte sighed. "It's funny, but I don't feel her here. I mean, I know her body is in here, but I just don't feel her presence. But when I'm walking down the street, I'll hear her voice, see her face. She'll be right there, as real as you are."

"So you're still hearing voices, then?" Jules looked at her sympathetically.

"I'm not 'hearing voices.' She is actually talking to me. I am not making it up. Don't look at me like you think I'm insane."

"Okay, okay, she's talking to you. So how's the father figure?"

"It's bizarre, kind of like living with an annoying roommate you have no choice about. Remember Joe?"

When they were in their junior year of college, finally allowed to move off campus, Jules had found them two rooms in a ramshackle three-bedroom apartment a few blocks away from school. They always said that the guy who sublet to them, Joe, a social geography major, had the personality of a serial killer.

He was quiet, kept to himself, but I'm not surprised, Charlotte always imagined saying to the police during the interrogation after they found the bodies of all the strangled co-eds in Joe's overcrowded-with-corduroy closet. On nights when Jules, who had more of an active social life, slept elsewhere, Charlotte would prop a chair in against her door for protection.

For the most part, Charlotte had loved college. Although she felt guilty sometimes, it was wonderful being away from her mother and having no responsibilities besides homework and a part-time job at the food co-op, packaging hummus and tahini. To pay for school, she had gotten a full scholarship and work-study, and if she wasn't working or studying in her favorite carrel in the library, she could be found hanging out with Jules on the Quad, a small grassy space that bisected the minuscule campus.

"He was disgusting," said Jules. "Remember how he used to leave a clump of hair in the drain every time he showered? It was like a small animal."

"Or a toupée. He was revolting," agreed Charlotte.

"Hey, Charlotte, does anyone else have a key to this place?"

"Just Mr. Sneed. I went by his office to pick it up. Why?"

"Just curious. How is the old codger?"

"Fine. You know, Jules, she knew," said Charlotte, sipping the last of her wine.

"Knew what? What are you talking about?"

"Corinne. She knew she was sick. Mr. Sneed told me."

"But I thought it was the sculpture. That it was a sudden heart attack."

"Mr. Sneed said he hadn't wanted to upset me, and she didn't want me to know, but the doctors had told Corinne that she probably had a clot."

"You're kidding!"

"They told her she needed to get an operation right away, but she wanted to finish her sculpture. She never used to go to doctors. She didn't trust them. I was always after her to get a checkup. I guess she finally did, but she didn't tell me about it. It's weird how you start remembering all this stuff. She used to get light-headed sometimes, and she said she thought it was the chemicals she was working with, but maybe it was her heart. I think she didn't care. Maybe she even wanted to die."

"Charlotte, that's ridiculous, your mother didn't want to die."

"I should have been paying more attention," said Charlotte,

picking up tiny pieces of bread that were scattered on the floor around Jules. "I could have helped her. I could have given her remedies, made her take care of herself."

"There was nothing you could have done." Jules stood up, stepping around Charlotte, doing a tour around the tiny space.

"I guess," said Charlotte, unconvinced.

"Hey, do you realize that this room is the size of a small New York apartment? She must have paid a fortune for this. It could even be a tiny studio. We could condo it. I could see the listing at Corcoran's: *Charming stone detail, cozy, perfect starter apartment.*"

"Don't people usually want a window, and a kitchen, and maybe a bathroom?"

"Okay, it's a fixer-upper."

Charlotte buttoned her cardigan. "It's freezing in here."

"It's nice. It's hot as hell outside."

It *was* nice inside the mausoleum, in a kind of morbid way. The floor was cool and dark, the walls a smooth dark stone. They finished their sandwiches and the rest of their wine and then stretched out on the floor of the mausoleum, as much as they could stretch out in the tiny space, making pretend snow angels on the cold floor.

"I think I'd like to be in here too," said Charlotte. "I wonder if there's room for me." They looked around. There was only one drawer carved into the wall, but there was clearly room for more.

"I think it might get a little depressing, and you'd definitely have to do something about the lighting. I can see a whole Goth thing going on: velvet armchairs, weird medieval hangings, some Day of the Dead paraphernalia."

"No, I mean when I die."

"You really want to be in here with your mother?"

"You said it yourself—it's nice in here. Cool. Peaceful."

"Okay, here it is," said Jules, reading from the brochure. " 'The preconstructed vestibule mausoleum provides for interment of one to six family members.' What about your father?"

"He probably wants to get buried with Hank Williams. He is obsessed with country music."

"That's cool. My father is obsessed with Andrew Lloyd Weber, and there's nothing worse than that."

"We'd better get back," Jules continued.

"Wait. I want to leave something. I almost forgot." Charlotte rummaged in her bag. "I brought something for her to read." She pulled out a battered paperback and laid it gently on the floor of the mausoleum.

Jules picked up the book by the cover.

"*The Fountainhead*. I always hated Ayn Rand. I mean, why does she pronounce her name in that stupid way, not like *Anne*, but *Ay-en*. And wasn't she totally politically incorrect?"

"She's here. I think I heard her."

"Ayn Rand?"

"No, my mother. She's here."

"Charlotte, have you ever thought of going to see a shrink? I think you've been playing that role-playing game too long."

"Wait, no, she's gone."

※

That night, Charlotte couldn't sleep. At three in the morning, she was wide awake. In the weeks since her mother's death, this was not uncommon. She had tried chamomile tea, valerian, hops, meditating. Nothing worked. She hated the middle of the night. It was too dark, too quiet, too full of danger. She went into the kitchen to get some water and take some Calms Forte, a homeopathic sleep remedy. While she was waiting for the tiny pills to melt under her tongue, she noticed movement in a corner of the dark living room and froze.

"Charlotte," a voice said. It was William.

"Oh my god, you scared me."

"I'm sorry. I was trying to be quiet."

"What are you doing?"

William was sitting with his cowboy boots up on the coffee table. He began strumming softly on his old beat-up guitar. "Can't sleep."

"Me too."

"I was thinking about your mother. I want to be angry at her, but I can't."

This was the first time it occurred to Charlotte that William had his own feelings about her mother. That maybe she hadn't treated him that well either. She wanted to ask him why he was angry with her. A thought came to her.

"Didn't you ever read about Corinne? I mean, she wasn't always famous, but in the last few years she has been in the press, at least the art press. Didn't you ever read that she had a daughter and add two and two together?"

William looked at her, embarrassed. "I wish I could say I did, but I didn't."

"Do you even feel like you're my father? Maybe you aren't. Maybe it's all a mistake."

William looked at her with the same blue-gray-green eyes she saw staring at herself in the mirror every morning.

"I don't think it's a mistake, Charlotte."

Charlotte started clearing up everything on the coffee table: potato chips, old crossword puzzles, glasses. Charlotte noticed that he did the crossword puzzle in ink, and was a little impressed in spite of herself.

"I'll do that," said William, picking up a plate.

"No, it's okay. I'll do it," said Charlotte, trying to take the plate from him.

They stood there glaring at each other for a moment, each holding one side of the plate, and then each put it back down on the table, giving up. They both sat down on the couch, leaving all the stuff exactly where it was.

"Do you mind if I turn on the TV?"

Charlotte shook her head, then got up and sat down on the chair farthest away from him. She couldn't bear the thought of lying on her bed watching the ceiling tonight.

Almost against their wills, they started watching celebrity profiles on the E Channel together. It was *Breakfast Club* week, so they watched Molly Ringwald, then Ally Sheedy. Charlotte and William were both mesmerized in spite of themselves.

"I've always liked Molly Ringwald," said William, sheepishly.

"Me too. Did you see *Sixteen Candles*?"

"Of course."

"I think that was her best movie."

"What about *Pretty in Pink*?"

"I can't believe you saw that. I liked it, except for that hideous prom dress she made."

After Anthony Michael Hall's segment, Charlotte started to feel incredibly sleepy. She looked at the clock, and unbelievably, it was five-thirty in the morning. She had to get up in two hours. She got up to go to bed.

"That was fun, but hopefully we won't have to do this again too soon," said William, yawning.

Charlotte fell asleep as soon as her head hit her orthopedic pillow. She woke up to the sound of birds.

She made coffee for the two of them, although she figured William probably wouldn't get up for hours.

I'm glad you and your father are getting along. He's not so bad, is he?

Then why did you dump him?

It's complicated.

Charlotte went back over to the couch, picking up an errant beer can. "He is a slob," she said, but no one was listening.

Her mother was gone and she was starting to feel like Felix in the Odd Couple.

She thought of them watching the show about *The Breakfast Club* together. She liked that movie. Charlotte had always liked to watch movies about teens, probably because she had never had any kind of normal teenagehood. Corinne was always dragging her from place to place and she never had time to make friends and settle in. She wasn't picked on in school, but she was never totally accepted either. Until she met Jules, she had never had a true best friend.

Chapter Nine

WHEN CHARLOTTE FINALLY got up the courage to call Colin, he was too busy to meet with her for almost two weeks. She had almost given up hope of ever rehearsing her scene when he finally called her and arranged a meeting.

Colin worked as a bartender, mostly on the weekends, so he was only free to meet Charlotte and rehearse during the day. When she was with him, she felt a pure sharp happiness. If someone had asked her if she had been happy before—before acting, before her father appeared, before her mother died—she would have said yes, she had been happy, but now she was beginning to wonder if she'd been half asleep the whole time.

They met for the first time at a diner on West Third Street. Over strawberry-rhubarb pie, she found herself trying to explain the concept of homeopathy to him.

"It doesn't really make any logical sense, but it works."

"How?" asked Colin, pouring heavy cream over his pie.

"Well, one of the major ideas of homeopathy is the law of infinitesimals. Basically, that means less is more. The smaller the amount of a homeopathic remedy, the more powerful it is."

Colin nodded. He seemed genuinely interested, but maybe he was this way with everyone.

She found herself watching his hands as he played with a sugar packet. He was addicted to sugar, pouring packet after packet into his tea. He never drank coffee. He finished his pie and turned the conversation away from homeopathy and back to his career, but she hadn't really been listening to him, just listening to the lilting sound of his Irish accent that made every word sound like a touch, until it finally got through to her that he was upset.

"I had an agent for a while," said Colin, "but he turned out to be useless. I wasted a year on that idiot."

"I'm sorry," said Charlotte, wishing that she had the power to magically cast Colin in a Broadway play. She asked him about his childhood.

He came from a family of eight. Grew up in Belfast. They were Catholic. He went to Catholic school, was briefly an altar boy, was slightly tortured at the hands of sadistic nuns. He was the next to youngest, had four brothers who still lived in the town they grew up in, all married with kids, one sister who lived in Scotland and one who lived outside of London.

"What made you come here?" asked Charlotte.

"I've always wanted to live in New York. I probably got it from the movies. *Saturday Night Fever. The Godfather.* It just seemed the place to be." He smiled and drank more tea.

At seven o'clock, he suddenly had to leave. Charlotte didn't care; she was glad of the chance to be alone and go over every aspect of their meeting in her mind.

When she got back to the loft, Charlotte was confronted by voices: William's deep voice and the twins' higher, squeakier ones.

"Charlotte, we've been waiting for you," the twins chimed together. "Where have you been?"

Charlotte suddenly remembered that she had invited the twins over for dinner. She was supposed to meet them at the loft at six. She couldn't believe she had forgotten. "We got you this great fondue set," said Sophie, waving a red metal fork around like a magic wand.

"Don't worry, Charlotte, I'm going to clean this up," said William.

"Drink," said Lauren, shoving a glass of red wine into Charlotte's hand.

William and the twins were standing around the kitchen table, drinking wine, acting like old friends, poking their metal forks into the sticky cheese concoction. The kitchen was a mess, grated cheese and bread crumbs and bottles of liqueur everywhere. Even though it was her house and her father, for a moment Charlotte felt like the outsider. The twins had a way of taking people over, and for some reason she didn't want them to take over William. Stop being ridiculous, Charlotte, she told herself. You invited them over.

"So, how's work?" she asked Sophie. The twins did something mysterious at a well-known investment bank.

"The usual: meetings, conference calls, lunch, meetings," answered Lauren.

"Today we went to a meeting and we were supposed to present our spreadsheet, but Lauren clicked on the wrong button and she deleted it, can you believe it? What a loser."

Lauren laughed, unconcerned. "Screw you, it all worked out anyway."

They offered Charlotte a slim metal fork, with which she speared a piece of French bread, dipping it into the bubbling cheese.

The cheese burned the roof of her mouth but tasted delicious. "Wow, this is really good."

"Thank William, he did most of the work."

"The secret is a little kirsch," said William proudly.

"So how's it going, this whole living-together thing?" said Sophie, obviously a little drunk.

Charlotte didn't say anything.

William finally offered, "It's an adjustment, but we're working on it."

Lauren wandered around the apartment with her glass of wine. "Our room isn't here anymore, is it?"

Charlotte shook her head. "No, she moved things around. There are only two bedrooms now."

"That's sad," said Sophie.

"It's so weird to be here without Corinne," said Lauren.

Sophie dropped her piece of focaccia into the cheese and said, "Okay, now I get to make a wish. That's the rule."

"Don't tell us what it is or it won't come true," said Charlotte.

"You're so superstitious, Charl."

"Lauren was just telling me about your childhood," said William.

"Don't believe anything they tell you." She turned to the twins, shaking her head at them. "I still can't believe I forgot about our date—I'm really sorry."

"Don't sweat it," said Lauren. "We've been having a great time. You know, I forgot how much I love this neighborhood, all the cool little stores and the restaurants. Maybe we should move here."

The twins owned a condo in a full-service high rise in the East Seventies.

"I don't know, I think Broadway is becoming sort of like a strip mall," said Sophie. "Did you see they have a huge Victoria's Secret now? That shouldn't be allowed."

"I stick to the side streets," said Charlotte.

"You know what we should do," said Sophie, trying to pour out wine from the empty bottle. "Go out and have a drink."

"Fabulous idea," said Lauren. They both chanted, "Change of venue! Change of venue!"

"I don't know, do you really think it's a good idea?" said Charlotte.

"I'm dying for a cosmopolitan—do you have any Grey Goose?" asked Lauren, opening the freezer door.

"No, we don't have any Grey Goose, whatever that is."

"It's vodka, silly, how about Ketel One?"

"No. All right, all right. I get the message. I'm ill-equipped for entertaining. We can go for a drink if you want." Charlotte was hoping William wouldn't come along, but of course the twins insisted.

Sophie pulled Charlotte aside in the elevator as they were waiting for Lauren and William. "He's really cute."

"Sophie, you are disgusting. He's old enough to be your father."

"He's *your* father," crowed Sophie.

"Believe me, I am painfully aware of that fact."

"But that doesn't mean he isn't an eligible bachelor. I bet Lauren is already sinking her claws into him. Lauren," Sophie called out across the loft. "Where the hell are you?"

Lauren and William emerged from the back of the loft, flushed and laughing.

At the bar, Charlotte ordered a vodka and soda, a drink her mother used to order sometimes. The twins had cosmopolitans, pink, frothy concoctions in large martini glasses.

"One vodka and soda coming up." William handed her the drink, and Charlotte handed him a ten, which he pushed back at her.

"Don't be silly, Charlotte."

She drank her vodka and soda. William had a scotch.

Charlotte sat at the bar, playing with the straw in her second vodka and soda. She looked around at the dark walls, the dark wood paneling, the other people in the room sitting by themselves. She imagined herself an old lady, coming to a bar every night for companionship, drinking to forget about everything. She would be one of those scary old ladies people move away from when they come into the bar until the bartender tells them, *Don't worry about her, she's harmless.*

Sophia and Lauren were playing pool in the back with William. They waved for her to come over, but Charlotte stayed glued to her bar seat. Lauren came over and sat on the barstool next to her.

"William's okay," she said.

"You're not really interested in him, are you?"

"I would be if he wasn't practically a relative."

"Lauren, please don't. . . ."

"All right. If you say so, sis. He doesn't happen to have any money, does he?"

"No, he's penniless."

"Well, Sādāt's Sādāt, as they say in Egypt."

After a third drink, Charlotte claimed a headache and everyone headed home.

Later, Jodee called her to ask her how her scene study was going and to complain about her partner. They were doing a scene from *Stage Door.* "I just know Heather's going to drag me down."

"She does seem a little eccentric."

"Did I tell you that my father is thinking of funding a showcase for me?"

"No. That's great."

"I know. I need to be out there. How's the scene going with Colin?"

Charlotte thought about that first meeting with him. How she had felt like Sheherazade trying to entertain him with stories so he wouldn't leave, how the room seemed smaller once he sat down across from her, how he leaned in very close to her when she spoke.

"Great. It's going great."

Charlotte and Colin were meeting twice a week now, usually in the Village. On the days she was going to see him, she couldn't eat anything. She would change her outfit three or four times, often ending up with the original one. They would, depending on the meeting place, drink coffee, eat lunch or have a drink, and most of the time run through some of their lines. Rushing out of work to arrive at their meeting place early, she would always end up waiting for him. He had the knack of arriving just at the moment when she had begun to doubt that he would show up at all. But then he would kiss her on the cheek and be so charming that it was impossible to be angry with him.

He told her stories about his bartending job at a seafood restaurant in the Union Square area, stories about obnoxious after-work groups who barely left a tip, women who came on to him. He was particularly disdainful of the aggressive women and particularly sympathetic to the drunks.

"You should come over one night. I'll buy you a drink."

"I'd like that," said Charlotte, wondering if he was serious.

They read lines from the scene.

Charlotte loved to hear the sound of his voice, his Irish accent. It made her think of hot baths, buttered toast, fields of heather.

He said the accent hurt him in auditions. "They like it, but they only want me to play the Irish git or the drunk at the bar."

He was getting coached in American dialects and he asked Charlotte for advice on how to pronounce certain words or how to use slang. She told him not to say brilliant if he meant great.

Sometimes she would have to remind him that they had to work on the scene. Often, just as they had gotten started rehearsing, Colin would rush off to work or an audition, leaving Charlotte wandering around the Village hearing his melting voice in her ears.

He always paid for her, despite her protests. "You'll have me over for a meal sometime, Charlotte, that'll make up for it."

Jodee called her frequently, ostensibly to talk about class.

"So, what did you think of that exercise with Susan? What's with that fake British accent anyway? Speaking of accents, how's our charming Irish friend?"

"He's good, but I'm kind of nervous about doing the scene with him. I don't want to make a fool of myself."

"It must be nice to work with someone talented and male. Heather just critiques me all the time."

In class, Colin pulled Charlotte aside to give her his thoughts about *Summer and Smoke*.

He wanted to have her think about the weather in the scene. "I see it as hot and damp, Charlotte, like the weather right before a storm."

After he spoke with her, she felt special, singled out. Now that she was in the scene with Colin, there was a difference in how the other students interacted with her. She had become cool by association. The students confided in her: the girls about their bulimic tendencies, breast implants, bad character choices; the guys about their auditions, bad girlfriend and boyfriend choices.

After class, one of the guys came up to her and asked, "Is it true that Colin was in the IRA?"

For a moment Charlotte couldn't figure out what Colin would have to do with financial planning, but then she realized that he was talking about the Irish Republican Army. She couldn't believe he was asking her that. She said, "That would explain the dynamite in the fridge."

The guy raised his eyebrows knowingly. "I guess you couldn't say even if he was. So what did you think of my scene?"

"Nice work," said Charlotte.

✽

Over dim sum in Chinatown, she asked Colin about her character, what he thought about her motivation, her emotional touch points, all the things she was hearing about in class.

He flagged down a passing waitress and ordered more shrimp sui mai. "Charlotte, to be honest, I don't go in for all this method crap. I pay lip service to it, but I think that all you have to do is stop thinking and act. You're doing fine, by the way."

"But we haven't even read through the whole scene."

"All right, this Thursday night. We'll do it. I'm off at the restaurant. We'll do a full run-through. The whole bloody thing." He took out an ancient-looking leather date book that Charlotte found endearing. "Where do you live?"

She told him. "Are you sure—"

"I'd say we could meet at my place, but my roommate and I aren't exactly getting along so well. You're not married, are you?"

"No." Charlotte was flattered that he thought she might be.

"Good. Then I'll see you Thursday. Eight o'clock."

The rest of the week, Charlotte felt like she was floating.

She researched bizarre head injuries at work, including a true story of a woman who had gotten mangled by a bear on a camping trip. She learned that if a bear is chasing you, you should not run up a tree, because the bear will go up after you. You should not make eye contact with the bear. Months after the incident, after undergoing multiple surgeries and painful treatments, the woman's husband, who also had been mangled by the bear, actually wanted to go camping again, face his fears. The couple got a divorce.

Tom, the disaster maven, told her a story about how more and more sharks were biting people. When you see a shark, as opposed to a bear, you are supposed to fight back, ideally by poking it in the eye with a sharp object, if you have one handy, he told her. Apparently sharks don't really want to eat people. They really prefer fish. They just try humans out to see if they are tasty, the way people bite into chocolates and put them back into the box.

In the afternoon, a woman came into the library. She had heard that Charlotte prescribed remedies.

Charlotte shook her head. "No, I just look up information on-line. What do you need?"

The woman, dark-haired and nervous, mid-forties, confided in a low voice, "I am afraid I have breast cancer."

"Have you been diagnosed?"

"No, but five of my friends have had it. I live in Long Island. I come from Ashkenazi Jews. I can't stand it. I've had ultrasounds, mammograms, biopsies. Nothing. The doctors, I know they're missing something."

Charlotte didn't know what to tell her. They could be missing something, but somehow she didn't think so. "I can't do anything about diagnosing cancer, but I really think that you're probably fine. I can recommend something for the fear and the anxiety. How are you sleeping?"

"I'm not."

"Try this," said Charlotte, pressing some of her special sleep remedy into the woman's hand. "Put four pills under your tongue before you go to bed."

After work, Charlotte stopped by Dean & Deluca, a gourmet store in the Village. She bought goat cheese studded with peppercorns, a crusty French baguette, some Belgian chocolates, grapes and a tomato.

Was she trying too hard? Would he think she thought that it was a date? And what should she wear? When she got home, she looked at the red sundress of her mother's and decided against it. She needed new clothes. Her clothes were so ordinary, so boring. All the women in acting class wore tight little T-shirts and jeans, or dresses that looked like costumes. The majority had tattoos, on their ankles, on the napes of their necks or hovering right above the backs of their low-riding jeans. There were also a number of piercings: eyebrows, navels, who knew what else. Charlotte didn't want a tattoo, but ever since her hair started to grow in after her haircut, she had started to feel as if she was disappearing again, after being visible for a brief moment. She would have to get Jodee, queen of miniature clothing, to take her shopping.

Charlotte settled on a pair of black stretch pants she wore for ballet class and a loose black sweater. She put on a little makeup and then wiped most of it off.

⸙

Colin was supposed to come over at eight o'clock. William had left her a note saying he was going out for the evening, which was perfect timing. It was kind of comforting to have someone there, just in case of emergencies and serial killers, but now, with Colin in the picture, she wished she lived alone. William had gotten a job at a local gallery that was doing some renovation at night to get ready for a big show. He seemed to have had a lot of these temporary jobs over the years, had never really settled into anything.

Charlotte had asked Mr. Sneed if he knew whether William had any family. She told herself that she didn't want aunts and uncles and cousins showing up at her doorstep. Mr. Sneed had told her that he didn't know, that she should ask William.

She didn't really care about his family, but it did seem strange that he was so completely on his own. She wanted to ask him about it, but she didn't want to seem too interested.

Colin was late as usual, ringing the bell loudly at eight forty-five. Even though Charlotte had been pacing around the kitchen waiting for him, when the bell actually rang the noise startled her. She waited for the elevator and opened the heavy door for him.

He smiled and gave her a kiss. On the cheek. She could tell by his smile that he approved of her living situation. He walked around the loft as if it were an apartment he was pacing out to determine the square footage.

"This is brilliant—I mean, great."

Charlotte smiled and watched him stride around the apartment, picking up a snow globe, putting it down, picking up a CD of William's, putting it down. She could see him living here. He'd fit in better than she, with his tight blue jeans and leather jacket and boots that he wore all the time, even in the summer. She tried to conjure up a vision of them living here together, plays and books and scripts strewn all over the floor, scones in the kitchen, his socks by her bed.

Suddenly he was right next to her. "Could I trouble you for something to drink, Charlotte?"

"Of course. How rude of me. I should have offered you something. Beer, wine, ginger ale?" Charlotte opened the refrigerator to display the beers. William had some Rolling Rocks, and she had bought a couple of exotic brands in case Colin was picky.

"I'd love a beer, although I didn't take you for a beer drinker," said Colin, grabbing a Boddington's. Charlotte took it from him and poured it into a glass.

"Or a guitar player, for that matter," he said, picking up the old acoustic lying on the couch.

"I'm not. The beer and the guitar belong to my father. He's staying here for a little while."

"He must be all right, then. Does your mum live here too?"

"No, she's . . . she . . ." Charlotte couldn't get out the words. For a moment she wasn't even sure where her mother was.

Finally she said, "My mother was a sculptor, Corinne Stiles. She had an accident. She died. This was her loft."

"I'm so sorry, Charlotte. I didn't know." He put his hand over hers and it felt so heavy and warm and wonderful, she wanted it to stay there forever.

He took a sip of beer, releasing her hand. "You poor thing. It's nice of you to stay and keep your father company."

It seemed important to Charlotte that he know they weren't a real family. "They weren't married. Actually, I just met him, my father. I grew up with my mother. It's complicated."

Colin looked at her with increasing interest. "Charlotte, you have hidden depths, you do."

Charlotte couldn't help feeling pleased at his assessment. "We really should get started on the scene."

"All right."

They moved over to the couch and started reading their lines.

Charlotte was hyper-aware of the closeness of his blue-jeaned leg to her black stretchy one. He kept shifting around restlessly, moving closer, then farther away.

In the scene, Colin's character, Johnny, was trying to lead her character astray. At one point in the scene, he takes her hand, and when they were reading that part, Colin really took her hand, wrapping his fingers around hers tightly. Charlotte didn't know what to do with her hand inside his and forgot to say her lines for a moment. She was afraid her hand was clammy and shaking and he would know how nervous she was. She tried to see her hand as Alma's hand, small and frail and sexually repressed.

His hand was gone much too soon, although there was a certain relief to having it gone.

"'Some women are called frigid,'" said Johnny, reading his lines.

Charlotte looked ahead a few lines while Johnny was talking, putting her finger on the part of the scene where he was supposed to kiss her, the part they had never rehearsed.

Then she said her line, "'Do I give that impression?'"

This was the point where the stage directions said to kiss her.

Colin pretended to lift her veil.

He leaned in gently, pressing his lips to hers.

There was a stage direction to kiss her again.

He kissed her again, with slightly more pressure.

After the kiss, they continued reading the scene as if nothing had happened, but Charlotte's lips were still tingling.

Alma and Johnny fight in the scene, and finally Alma gets angry and moves away from him.

When they finished, Colin said, "You're good. You're the perfect Alma."

Charlotte wasn't sure if that was a compliment. She was a perfect version of an uptight, sexually repressed spinster hypochondriac in love with her doctor and childhood friend, now a ne'er-do-well gambler and womanizer.

"Thanks."

"What did you think about the kiss?" he asked, sitting next to her again, his leg pressed against hers.

Charlotte didn't know what to say,

Colin answered his own question. "I think it worked. We'll have to practice it, though."

"I'll have to get a veil so you can pull it up."

"I can't wait."

"Are you hungry?" asked Charlotte, not looking at him.

"Famished."

Charlotte put out the food and got Colin another beer, pouring herself a glass of wine, although she didn't ordinarily drink much, not wanting to become an alcoholic like her mother.

They ate and talked about the studio: who was doing what scene, who they thought had talent.

"What do you think of Jodee?" asked Charlotte.

"She's all right. Cute. Good for a soap, maybe."

She wondered if Jodee was his type.

They ran through the scene two times more, just the lines, not the movements.

The third time they ran through it, Charlotte said her last Alma line—" 'You are not a gentlemen' "—and glared at Colin/Johnny.

Someone clapped and they both turned around and saw William standing at the door. "Very nice," he said.

Colin stood up and took a long exaggerated bow from the waist.

"Colin, this is William."

After an awkward handshake, they all sat down again at the kitchen table and ate the rest of the food.

"Charlotte was telling me about your unusual situation here," Colin said to William, breaking off a hunk of baguette and covering it with goat cheese.

"We are just starting to get to know each other," said William, smiling at Charlotte, who tried to ignore him while she carefully examined the pieces of chocolate.

"Charlotte, I'm sorry I had to interrupt your rehearsal, but my job got cut short."

"It's okay," said Charlotte, thinking the opposite.

"Where are you working?" asked Colin.

William told Colin about his job at the gallery. "It's just temporary. I'm thinking of taking up painting again or going to cooking school."

Colin asked him about what he'd been doing before. Charlotte tried not to look interested. William described a series of jobs—handyman, carpenter, short-order chef. "Anything that needed doing." He'd done them in some interesting places: "Tahoe, Key West, Jackson Hole, Venezuela."

"Wow," said Charlotte.

"I've always been meaning to settle down, but it just never happened."

"Any other kids besides Charlotte?" asked Colin innocently.

Charlotte focused on the olives, arranging them in concentric circles, all the while listening for William's answer. What if he did have another child? What would that mean? Or more than one? She could have a slew of brothers and sisters, scattered around the country like pins on a map.

William sounded annoyed. "No, how about you?"

Colin laughed but didn't answer the question.

Charlotte felt relieved at William's response, but was still curious. She turned to him and asked, "What about your family, your parents? You never said anything about them."

"There's not that much to tell. I'm an only child, my parents retired up in Vancouver—I see them maybe once a year."

"Did you tell them about me?" asked Charlotte.

"No, not yet, but I would like to, eventually, if that's okay with you."

"I guess," said Charlotte, trying to imagine having grandparents, a new concept. Corinne's parents had died when she was very young, and Corinne had been estranged from them long before that.

After every crumb of baguette and every grape was eaten, William said, "I should be turning in."

William stood in front of Colin until Colin said, "It was very nice meeting you." Standing and shaking William's hand, he added, "I should get going too. Charlotte—or should I say Alma—I'll see you on Tuesday." He gave her a brief peck on the cheek and then disappeared.

Charlotte was alone with William. Why couldn't *he* have left? Why did he have to chase Colin away? She felt like crying out of frustration and anger.

"Interesting guy," said William in a way that suggested he thought Colin might be an ax murderer.

"Yes, he's a very good actor."

"I'll bet," said William, tossing the beer cans into the recycling basket that Charlotte had set up.

"Good night," said Charlotte, although she knew he wanted to stay and ask her more questions about Colin. She started walking toward her room.

"No celebrity bios tonight?"

She turned around and answered, "No, I'm kind of tired."

"I think *St. Elmo's Fire* is on."

"Some other time."

As she was starting to close the door of her room, William called out, "Hey, Charlotte, are you going to be performing that scene you were doing with Colin? In front of an audience?"

"Yes," said Charlotte, wanting to take it back as soon as she said it.

"You'll have to let me know when it is. I'd love to come."

"Okay. Good night." Charlotte shut the door to her room and lay on her bed, but she couldn't transport herself back to the moment of Colin kissing her. The presence of her father kept intruding. Her father strumming on the guitar, her father painting in the loft, her father kissing her mother, loving her mother, leaving her mother. She didn't want him coming to her show, pretending he was her father. She wished she had some of the sleeping tablets Alma kept taking in the play.

She lay there, wide awake. There was nothing more she wanted to do than go out and watch mindless television in the living room, but not with William.

For weakness of will, try Centaury.

Chapter Ten

THE NEXT DAY on her lunch hour, Charlotte met Jules and they went out shopping for sperm.

"I didn't know what to wear," said Jules. "I want to seem available but not slutty."

"I don't think the sperm can see you," said Charlotte.

"You never know."

When they got to the sperm bank, it had the hushed, confidential feel of a dating service. Jules filled our countless forms and answered the counselor's personal questions, and after a long wait they were given a huge loose-leaf folder with potential candidates to pick from. Jules was disappointed they didn't have pictures.

"I like number 27227: green eyes, brown hair, good SAT scores," said Jules.

"Don't you think it is a little weird of him to put down his SAT scores?"

"He's probably only eighteen years old, what else has he done? Anyway, I always liked the idea of a younger man."

"I rehearsed with Colin last night."

"And . . . ?"

"Well, he kissed me, in the scene."

Jules looked up from the files, raising her eyebrows. "And how was it?"

Charlotte thought about it. "It was nice, very nice."

"Maybe he has some extra sperm he'd like to donate. I could save five thousand dollars."

"Wow, it's expensive. And no, you can't have his sperm."

"Thanks for sharing. And that's just the sperm. What about babyGap, pediatricians, day care, therapy, Ritalin? The list goes on and on."

"How are you going to pay for it?"

"Well, I've got a plan. I'm going to write about each stage and sell the articles. And I've already got a deal in the works for a single-mother book. Single motherhood for dummies, that kind of thing."

"I could help out, babysit . . ."

"I will definitely take you up on it. But I thought you weren't interested in kids."

"I think I would be a terrible mother, but a good aunt. If you have a child, can he come and visit me when I'm old and dying in a nursing home?"

"Sure, he'll come visit both of us. We'll make him stay for bridge and karaoke and embarrass the hell out of him."

"Thanks. Did I tell you that the acting class I'm in is putting on a show and I'm going to be in it?"

"Only a million times. No, seriously, that's great. Are there any nongay actors, besides your Irish guy, or any other potential sperm donors?"

"There's a couple."

"When is it?"

"Not for a couple of months. I'm sure I'll be a nervous wreck."

"So, he kissed you, huh?"

"It was in the script."

"So basically every time you rehearse, you are going to be kissing."

Charlotte smiled, not having considered this before, "Basically . . . at least if we do that part."

"Any tongue?"

"Jules!"

"It's a reasonable question."

"Let's get back to these guys here. And in answer to your question, no, there was no tongue."

"Yet," said Jules, poring over the sperm donors.

After they left the sperm bank and went their own ways, Jules having been unable to decide on a donor, Charlotte went back to work. She felt more energetic than she had in a long time.

When Tom came by with articles on the hanta virus, she filed them away without even looking at them. She felt happy, and except for one little nagging voice, everything would have been fine.

Charlotte.

I don't want to hear it.

I have more experience in these matters and I really think you should be careful. I went out with an Irish guy once.

You never cared when you were alive, so why should I listen to you now?

Charlotte, things have changed. I'm different now.

Right, and where are you, exactly?

I can't say, but I've changed.

I have to get back to work. I don't want everyone to think I'm crazy. Talking to myself and all.

With that bunch of nut-jobs, I don't think you have to worry about it.

I can see you've really changed. Go away.

***

Charlotte went back to work, but she was seething. Why couldn't her parents leave her alone, like they had done her whole life? Just let her be? How was anything romantic supposed to happen between her and Colin with William traipsing in, playing country music, and with her mother making her look crazy?

***

For the next rehearsal, Charlotte suggested meeting at Colin's apartment. To her surprise, he agreed.

Colin lived in a tiny one-bedroom in the Lower East Side. Even though he had said he had a roommate, once she saw the tiny room, she couldn't imagine it. Maybe some friend from home had been staying there for a few weeks and had just left. The only furnishings were a futon on the floor, a makeshift coffee table, a couple of chairs and some bookcases.

Charlotte wore her Alma dress to try to get into character.

Colin made her tea and they sat on his lumpy futon couch and drank it. Before they even got to rehearsing the play, he kissed her. He kissed her and she leaned back into the couch until something sharp stuck her. She reached behind her and under the pillow while he was still kissing her, and pulled out a corkscrew.

"Oh, let me get that. Are you all right?" asked Colin.

"I'm fine." Charlotte felt shy but happy.

He put away the corkscrew and the teacups and then came back to her on the couch, leaning his body over hers. She breathed him in and then he kissed her again.

"I love your hair, Charlotte. It's so soft."

"I like yours too." (What an idiot, Charlotte, *I like yours too.*)

He laughed softly and kissed her more, sliding his hand up under her shirt. She wondered what underwear she had put on. She had been trying to wear her more feminine underwear lately, had even bought a new bra in pink lace, but today she was pretty sure she was wearing an old ratty white bra. She wished her breasts were bigger, that she had worn perfume, gargled, had a bikini wax, liked her body.

He looked into her eyes and she felt like her body was melting. This was what they were always talking about in all those romance novels and magazine articles. This scary melting feeling. This was *l'amour.*

He kept looking at her for reassurance. He took off his shirt and looked at her, started unbuttoning her shirt and looked at her. When he touched her breasts, she closed her eyes. After a few moments of this, he said, "Don't you think we'd be more comfortable on the bed?"

It was difficult to keep the mood in the transfer from couch to bed. Charlotte held together the top of her shirt with one hand and followed him. He took her hand, which made it easier. He pulled back the covers on his bed, which was just a box spring on the floor. The bed was made, though, with yellow floral sheets and a maroon bedspread. He pulled back the covers with a flourish and invited her in.

"Miss Alma."

"Thank you, Doctor."

She got into the bed and lay there, smiling at him. She didn't feel like taking off her clothes yet. Colin seemed to sense how she felt, because he just drew her to him and held her. Then, slowly, his hands moved under her shirt. He lifted her arms and slid her shirt off over her head.

Charlotte nuzzled into him, hiding her nakedness against him. He pulled away so he could kiss her breasts. She could feel his penis against her stomach through his pants. Her hand reached down almost of its own accord and slid its way underneath his waistband. He inhaled sharply. "Why, Miss Alma."

He seemed to take her action as a sign that things could move much faster. He peeled off his pants and underwear and she slowly did the same. They were both naked now and she pulled the covers over both of them instinctively. She had gotten a glimpse of his body, though. He was very pale and slim. His penis looked large enough, but unthreatening—and uncircumcised, from what she could tell, a new experience for her. She also noticed his legs, which were surprisingly muscular, like a dancer's. She wanted to ask him if he had ever done Irish dancing. She had once watched an entire *Behind the Music* program about Michael Flatly, formerly of *Riverdance,* who was incredibly arrogant but a beautiful dancer. Colin reached into a drawer by the bed and grabbed a condom, unwrapping it expertly with one hand.

"Are you okay with this?"

Charlotte nodded. She was nervous, but this was exactly what she wanted.

He positioned himself over her and then slowly lowered into her. She liked the heavy feel of his weight. It was perfect. She had had sex before, but it had never felt this good. Colin kept whispering her name until she thought she would go crazy. She was moaning, making noises she had never heard from herself before.

Oh my god. This was it. She was actually having an orgasm. She couldn't wait to tell Jules.

Afterward, he carefully extracted himself and removed the condom, disposing of it discreetly and then lying back down next to her. She was breathing heavily, content.

"Lovely," said Colin, leaning over and kissing her lightly. She kissed him back.

He reached into the drawer by his bed and grabbed a pack of cigarettes. "Would you like one?"

Charlotte hadn't smoked since the one Balkan Sobranie of her mother's at the loft, but she nodded.

"I guess we're not going to rehearse today," said Colin, getting up and pulling on his pants. He stubbed out his cigarette in a Cinzano ashtray.

"Do you have to go to work?"

He sighed heavily. "Unfortunately."

Charlotte wanted to lie in the bed forever, pretending to smoke her Camel cigarette, but Colin looked like he was getting ready to leave, so she got up and pulled her clothes on quickly.

At the door, Colin gave her a kiss and said, "I'll call you."

Walking home, Charlotte kept repeating the event in her mind, as if to convince herself that it had really happened. I slept with Colin. I had sex with Colin. Colin and I had sex.

And what was going to happen now? She felt a combination of excitement and nausea at the prospect of the future. Was there going to be one, or was he going to act like it had never happened? When was he going to call her?

When she got home, she called Jules on her cell phone. Not in range.

She checked her e-mail. Nothing, just junk and a plaintive e-mail from Paul about Covington: "The darkness is spreading in Covington; your absence and crossbow have been sorely missed in The Dark Forest."

She felt guilty. It was true. Now that she had scene study and acting class, she hadn't been going to Covington as much. That was what she used to do practically every night: come home to Queens, eat a spinach pie and some tzatsiki and play the game for hours until she collapsed into bed, her wrist aching. She remembered weekends when she wouldn't even leave her apartment. She would read and play Covington and watch sad movies on the Lifetime Channel, movies about kidnappings, battered women, missing children. And the more time she spent inside, the harder it was to go out at all. It began to seem so much safer inside, away from all the noise and germs out there.

She logged on and met Paul in town. Ix was there, collecting his most powerful spells.

"You are here at an auspicious moment, Varlata, the creatures of evil are multiplying and the unicorn is weakening."

Charlotte quickly became engrossed in the game, killing monsters with deadly arrows, while Ix cast spells that froze them and drained off their energy.

After they cleared out an entire nest of sloth-vipers, they went back into town for a celebratory cyber-pint.

"No sign of the unicorn tonight, I'm afraid, but we have made the town safer."

"Another round of battle, perhaps?" asked Ix.

Varlata declined, storing her crossbow away in her locker. "No, I must go home, they are expecting me."

Off-line, she called Jules again.

"I had sex with Colin."

"What, I can't hear you, I'm on the street. Talk louder."

Charlotte felt like she was practically shouting. "I had sex with Colin."

"You're kidding me. The acting guy?"

"Yes."

"Oh my god! How was it?"

"Great."

"Did you . . . you know?"

"Yes."

Jules knew all about Charlotte's sexual inadequacies. Considering it a religious mission to help Charlotte, for years she had plied her with sex toys and pornographic videos at birthdays and Christmas, until Charlotte had begged her to stop.

For a while, Charlotte had dutifully watched the "made by women" videos and powered up the vibrators, but she would find herself focusing on something irrelevant, like the way the breast implants looked on a woman's chest, how they weren't quite placed in the right spot or looked like balloons, or the faces the men made, or how bad the acting was, and she would lose her momentum and stop, feeling embarrassed and ridiculous. The only hardcore porno film she had ever seen had so many close-ups it made her feel ill, like watching those medical shows where they show you the baby's head emerging all wet and glistening from a woman's vagina.

Charlotte knew medically what happened when you had an orgasm. Your blood pressure rose, your heartbeat accelerated and your breathing rate altered, and then, if you were lucky, you had a few blissful seconds of rhythmic muscular contractions. She had also researched orgasmic dysfunction, although she wasn't sure that was her problem. She had heard of homeopathic remedies for this problem, but she had never tried them. For loss of libido associated with grief or repressed emotions, there was *Natrum mur,* for indifference to sex, sepia.

Charlotte had never told Jules, but she had put all the sex toys and videos away in a box at the very top of her closet. The sound of the vibrator made her nervous, and the one time she had gotten close to orgasm, she had started worrying that it would malfunction and cause some permanent damage.

Maybe she had been brainwashed by reading too many romance novels when she was little, novels in which the heroine melts into the hero's arms and is made love to in a room surrounded by candles and firelight and fur throws. It just wasn't as romantic having sex with a vibrating plastic penis-shaped object.

"Way to go, Charlotte!" said Jules.

"Thanks," Charlotte felt proud, as if she had won something or joined an exclusive club.

"Is this a one-off thing, or are you two an item now?"

"I hope it's not just one time, but it's unclear at the moment."

"Don't let him walk all over you, Charlotte."

"I really like him, Jules."

"I know, Charlotte. But be careful. Did you use something?"

"Yes, perfectly safe sex."

"Any leftover sperm I could use?"

"You are disgusting."

Charlotte and Colin didn't have a rehearsal scheduled for two days. She would see him in class, though, in the morning, only a few hours away, although he hadn't said anything about it when they parted.

Charlotte got to the studio forty-five minutes early. Jodee was there, putting up flyers for the one-woman show she was doing. Colin wasn't there.

Charlotte couldn't focus on the class once it started. They were having a lecture from a guest speaker called "Streamline Your Life—Unleash Your Success!" To succeed as an artist, according to the speaker, your life had to be clutter-free. Bills had to be paid, surfaces cleared, emotional baggage stored away. Charlotte thought about the loft, all the garbage bags filled with her mother's possessions, the piles of unopened mail, the calls she had never returned.

She was tempted to ask the speaker what to do about a dead mother who keeps interfering in your life, talking to you.

The speaker described an additional course you could take in which she came to your house and decluttered and feng shuied you for five hundred dollars. Jodee had done it and now had candles and tinkling waterfalls all over her apartment.

"It really works," she whispered to Charlotte.

At the end of the lecture, Charlotte lingered by the podium, pretending to examine the pamphlet, while scanning the room for Colin. He's avoiding me, she thought. He never wants to see me again.

As she started to feel conspicuous and began to walk out of the room, she finally saw him, walking in the front door of the studio. Her legs felt heavy and she wanted to walk away from him, not toward him. She felt unkempt, awkward and tried not to look at him. He seemed to notice none of this and was actually walking right toward her.

"Audition," he whispered in her ear, giving her a kiss on the cheek, as if it were perfectly natural. "How was the lecture, the old clean-your-closets, get-a-part-in-a-movie rap?"

"It works," said Jodee, suddenly appearing between them like a jack-in-the box and smiling up at Colin under two layers of mascara. "You should try it."

"Right," said Colin skeptically. "Anyone up for some food? I'm starving. How about it, Charlotte?"

"Sure."

"Let's go," said Jodee.

Charlotte didn't know how to disinvite Jodee, so the three of them all went to a diner. Colin had a hamburger and french fries smothered in ketchup. Charlotte had a Greek salad. Jodee had a diet Coke with lemon, no ice, and all of Colin's leftover french fries, after he pushed them away.

Jodee talked nonstop during lunch. She was excited about her showcase and she gave them each a bundle of flyers to put around.

"It's called *I Slept with Keanu Reeves*. It's an extension of that scene I did in class last year where I danced around and talked about all my sexual experiences. How no one matches up to Keanu Reeves."

"Did you actually sleep with him?" asked Colin, smiling at Charlotte.

"Well, not exactly," admitted Jodee, "although I did see his band, Dogstar, once. They're pretty good."

"Do you think he can act, though?" asked Charlotte, who had loved *The Matrix* and seen it four times. "Sometimes he seems a little blank."

"That's his quality, his position statement—that openness."

"Let's face it," said Colin, "he's not all there. If he wasn't good-looking, he wouldn't have gotten anywhere."

Jodee looked horrified. "I still think he's a brilliant actor. *Devil's Advocate, Sweet November*. Those are classics."

"They're crap," said Colin.

"Do you know that his name means 'cool breeze over the mountains' in Hawaiian?" said Jodee reverently.

"So, what's the showcase about?" asked Charlotte.

"Well, it isn't really about him, it's about my fantasy of him. I wrote it all one weekend after I decluttered my life, and my father has a screenwriter friend he plays golf with who helped me edit it—oh, and Ron from The Craft is directing. It's about how every relationship doesn't match up to the fantasy."

"Just tell us when it is, we'll be there," said Charlotte, wondering if she should have said *we*.

"Are we rehearsing tomorrow?" asked Colin as they descended into the subway. "Your place?"

Charlotte nodded, wondering why he didn't want her to go back over to his house.

They separated to take different trains, Charlotte and Jodee heading downtown, Colin heading to work on the Upper West Side. On the subway, Jodee talked nonstop about Ron. "He's really cool. He's really helping with the play."

"Are you paying him?"

"No."

"Dating him?"

"Sort of. Speaking of that, is there something going on between you and Colin? I sensed something."

"I'm not sure," said Charlotte.

"Well, be careful, he's great and everything, but he seems really self-centered."

⟡

Later in the week, she ate a late dinner with Jules at Burger Palace. After having no luck at the sperm bank, Jules was flying off to China to look into the idea of adopting a Chinese baby. She had spent all her free time lately filling out forms, dealing with officials, trying to learn Chinese from Berlitz tapes.

"*Zao an,* that means good morning—wait, I really should be saying *wahn an,* which means good evening. You wouldn't believe the paperwork. It's like joining the FBI."

Charlotte played with her french fries.

"So, is there any advice you need before I go. About Colin, for example?"

"I really like him, Jules."

"More than Kenny?"

Kenny was a psych professor they both had had huge crushes on, and since then he had become the barometer for all love affairs.

"More than Kenny."

"Uh-oh. And how does he feel?"

"I don't know."

"It is great about the sex, though. I knew you could do it."

"Stop, you're embarrassing me."

"You know, now that it's working, the skill is transferable."

"Transferable?"

"Yes. You know, Charlotte, the ability rests with you, not him. You can have them with anyone."

Charlotte looked doubtful. "I guess."

"Well, not anyone, but trust me, now that you feel more comfortable, it will work with other people."

"I don't want it to work with other people. I just want it to work with Colin. You don't like him, do you?"

"I've never even met him."

"I'm going to miss you. Do they have phones in China?"

"Yes, all the mod cons. That's British for 'modern conveniences.'"

"Whatever, just call me."

Walnut is a protection remedy against powerful influences.

Chapter Eleven

CHARLOTTE AND HER father had taken to late-night television watching. After days of watching William watch TV while she sat in the kitchen pretending to read a book, Charlotte had gradually made her way closer and closer to him. First she stood near the couch, leaning down to see the set, then a few days later sat down on an uncomfortable wooden chair, and then finally one night she gave up and sat down on the other end of couch from him, telling herself it was only for a few minutes. Now, two or three nights a week, they would huddle in front of the small set watching the trashiest TV possible.

"I would have thought you were the Channel Thirteen type," said Charlotte, bringing a bowl of popcorn over to the coffee table.

"Actually, I used to watch the ten o'clock news and Charlie Rose religiously before I went to sleep, but then I discovered that although they can put you to sleep very effectively, later you get bad dreams. The E Channel, on the other hand, will put you to sleep for the duration. Anyway, after a while I began to realize that the reason I was watching television was because I wanted to escape, not to learn anything or to think too hard."

"Me too."

They watched old reruns of *Buffy the Vampire Slayer, Ally McBeal, E True Hollywood Stories, Legends and Scandals* and *Behind the Music.* The only thing they wouldn't watch were specials about Madonna, who they both felt, got way too much attention to begin with. Out of all the shows, *Buffy* was their favorite.

"I've always wanted to take martial arts," said Charlotte one night during a commercial break.

"I know a little aikido," admitted William.

Charlotte was impressed. "Could you show me?"

"Sure."

At the next commercial, William showed her how to use her attacker's momentum against them. He planted himself firmly, feet apart, and showed her how to move an attacker off balance or, in aikido-speak, how to use his qi (pronounced *chi*) against him. So, as William was coming toward her, pretending to be wielding a knife, she had to grab his arm above the wrist, and instead of fighting him, which was her natural reaction, she had to pull him toward her, on his own momentum, so he would lose his balance and she could get away.

When he grabbed her arm for the first time, it was strange— strange to think he was her father, that they shared strands of DNA. But after a moment, feeling the pressure of his hand made Charlotte angry. He should have known about me, she thought, he should have known.

"That was good, Charlotte, let's try it again."

She pulled her arm away. "Why did you and my mother split up?"

William seemed taken aback by the question. He sat down and took a long swig of his Rolling Rock. "Well, there were a lot of reasons. Your mother . . . well, it was difficult. We were both trying to pursue artistic careers, and initially your mother wasn't having much success. I was doing a little painting—figures, mostly—but then I got a small show, which got some good reviews. Your mother believed that it was much easier for men in the art world, that they got taken more seriously as artists, and after my show she started to resent me for it."

"She was right, about it being easier for men—not that I'm saying you weren't talented."

"It's okay. I know I never had the kind of talent your mother did. She always knew exactly what she wanted to create. Never doubted herself. But I wasn't bad."

"So what happened?"

"We started fighting. At first it all seemed so romantic. We didn't have any money. We worked odd jobs at restaurants or bars. For a while, she worked as a model for a life drawing class. We had a tiny apartment in the Village, on McDougal Street, over a Mexican restaurant. It was noisy and smelly, but it was as if we were living in Paris. We'd paint, we'd fight, we'd make up. But after I had my show, there began to be much more fighting than making up. It got pretty ugly." He paused. "I mean, physically ugly."

Charlotte didn't get what he meant, at first. What was he talking about? Who was physically ugly? Then she realized what he was trying to say. "You hit her?"

"Each other. And screamed. And broke things. Your mother broke my nose once," he said, fingering the bridge of his nose nostalgically. "You can't see it now, but it was quite a bump. Of course, there was always a lot of drinking."

"Of course," said Charlotte. For some reason, when he said the word *drinking* she flashed to a morning when she was eight years old. Her mother had been teaching down in Florida for a few months and had decided that Charlotte had been out of school long enough. She was afraid of Charlotte turning into a southern simpleton.

"Florida isn't really the South," her friends would argue.

But she was adamant. "Anywhere that serves those nasty wormy grits with your eggs is in the South as far as I'm concerned."

Corinne had gotten out of bed uncharacteristally early that morning and they slid into their cheap lime-green rental car and headed for the school. Her mother had a glass of what looked like orange juice in one hand and a cigarette on the other. "Just a little something to get me going," she told Charlotte confidentially, "a little tiny itsy-bitsy screwdriver."

She stowed the drink on the groove in the dashboard and started the car, cigarette dangling between her lips. When they got to the school, Charlotte looked at her mother's empty glass and knew this behavior was not normal. She saw the other mothers, dressed neatly in their khakis and pastel shirts, walking their children into the school, and felt a sharp stab of envy and shame. What she would have given for one of these boring PTA, Brownie troop–leader mothers. At the same moment, she realized she couldn't let her mother go in there. They would know just by looking at her. Convincing her mother to drop her off was easy. Inside, she had told her teacher that her mother was sick, that was why she hadn't come in, that a family friend had given her a ride.

William's voice brought her back into the present, to her relief. "The drinking was probably the real reason I left. And the fights. For a while after we split up, I stopped drinking altogether, went to meetings, did the whole AA thing. But as time went on, I realized that I was able to drink in moderation, that it was only the combination of the two of us that had been out of control."

Charlotte felt the old bitterness toward her mother. She said, "It was her. She was always out of control. And she never stopped drinking. If she had, maybe she wouldn't have died."

"You don't know that."

"I know that alcohol exacerbates health problems."

Something William had said struck Charlotte as strange. "But I thought she started drinking much later. Corinne always told everyone that after I was born, she went into a serious postpartum depression, and that drinking was the only way she could get off the pills they gave her."

"I'm sure she said that alcohol was the fuel of creativity too, but that doesn't mean it's true. And as for when she started drinking, Charlotte, the first night I met your mother—and I remember it distinctly—I impressed her with my margarita recipe and she impressed me with her ability to drink tequila."

"She talks to me." Charlotte had not meant to say that. The words just slipped out of their own accord. He was going to think she was insane.

William leaned his head in toward her as if trying to hear better. "Excuse me?"

Charlotte was speaking fast before she lost her nerve. "She talks to me. Out loud. It's really her. It's not my imagination. I was wondering if maybe she talked to you too."

William shook his head. "No, but why would she talk to me? We were over a long time ago. You are the one she has the connection with. It makes perfect sense that she talks to you, Charlotte."

"You believe me?"

"I've heard stranger things that turned out to be true."

Charlotte looked at William carefully. He didn't seem to be making fun of her or looking at her as if she was certifiable. Maybe he really believed her.

※

After their next class, Jodee and Charlotte went shopping for clothes. Jodie had grown on Charlotte, like a cute but hopelessly spoiled pet, the kind that always got fed human food in a special bowl. Charlotte was sick of all her clothes. They didn't fit her new life. She also wanted to look good for Colin, but she didn't tell Jodee that. Jodee took Charlotte to her "absolute favorite store" in the Village.

It was small, with blaring disco music, staffed by tall transvestites in high heels.

"All the clothes in here look like they're made for munchkins— no offense," said Charlotte, looking down at Jodee, who was only five-one.

"None taken. I like being little, it makes men feel so big. But don't worry," she said, "you have your own appeal."

"And what is that, exactly?"

Jodee peered intently at Charlotte as if looking into a crystal ball. "Classy, but with a hint of fire."

"You make me sound like someone in a soap opera."

"Don't you wish. It's simple, it's just like getting a part in a play. First you have to figure out your sexual position statement, and then you just have to dress and act the part."

"What's your sexual position statement?"

"I'm going for little, cute and slutty. You are classy but sexy."

Jodee pulled out a tiny one-size-fits-all T-shirt from a rack. "Here, try this on," she ordered. The T-shirt was a sparkly deep blue with a V-neck.

"Remember, men love glittering objects," confided Jodee. "I can't remember exactly what or why, but it does something to their brains."

Charlotte thought the tiny T-shirt would look ridiculous, but it was actually flattering when she tried it on.

Jodee opened up the curtain to her dressing room. "Can I come in?"

"You already are in."

Jodee had on a minuscule white leather skirt with fringe. "Too cowgirl?"

"Maybe," said Charlotte diplomatically.

"Hey, Charlotte, that shirt is fantastic on you—you have to get it!"

"Okay, okay."

"How about a miniskirt?"

"No, I don't think so."

When they came out of the dressing room, Charlotte was drawn to a vintage sweater trimmed in soft brown faux fur.

"Try it on. Men like things that are tactile: fur, leopard skin, velvet. It reminds them of prehistorical times when they were all hunters and shit."

"Speaking of men, how's Ron?" asked Charlotte, surprised that Jodee knew the word *tactile*.

Jodee groaned. "Just because he's directing my showcase and we slept together a couple of times, he thinks he's my boyfriend, and even worse, he never has any money. He thinks I should pay for myself." Jodee sounded outraged, as if she had been the victim of some horrible abuse.

"Men," sympathized Charlotte, in that aggrieved tone women use when they talk about men, just to agree with her.

"Hey, Charlotte, would you do me a big favor and help me out the night of the showcase?"

"Sure. What do you want me to do?"

"I don't know. Nothing much. Help me dress. Calm me down. Take some tickets, do a little ushering."

"I'd love to. Thanks for the shopping."

"I expect to see those clothes. Soon."

⸙

It took Charlotte a few days to get the courage to go out in her new clothes. She would try them on and take them off, thinking she looked ridiculous. Finally she just forced herself to put them on, even though she felt too exposed.

Seeing her come out of her room, William said, "Charlotte, you look very nice. Are you going out?"

"Actually, Colin is coming over here to rehearse."

"I see. He's from Ireland, right?" William said the word *Ireland* in a deeply suspicious way.

"Yes, Belfast."

"Well, you're in luck, Charlotte. I'm going out, so you can have the place to yourself."

Charlotte was curious. "Where are you going?"

"Some of the guys I was working with last week get together and play music every week. I'm going to jam with them."

Jam was such a ridiculous word for a man his age. Next he'd be gigging.

"So, how long do you think your rehearsal with Colin will last?"

"I don't know—midnight?"

"I'll try not to get home too early."

"Okay."

"Charlotte, there are some muffins in the fridge if you're interested: jalapeño-cheddar."

"Thanks." William was beginning to feel like a roommate, like the foreign exchange student she had lived with for a semester, who at first seemed impossibly strange, but imperceptibly had become part of the daily landscape. Someone you shared food with but tried to keep a certain emotional distance from because you knew they were eventually going back to their home country.

That night Charlotte stood in front of the fridge picking at a muffin, wondering where Colin was. The muffins were pretty good. Maybe Colin would want one later, if and when he ever got here. He said he'd come over at eight-thirty—but as nine and nine-thirty and ten and ten-thirty rolled around, still there was no Colin. Charlotte kept pacing, picking up her script and then putting it down. Finally, at 10:34, the phone rang. It was Colin. Apologizing, but not seeming all that apologetic. "Charlotte, I'm terribly sorry. You must hate me. I had to take care of something. It couldn't be helped. But we could still get together."

"My father will be home soon, so we wouldn't have any privacy."

"Do you want to come here?"

Charlotte felt angry, but said nothing.

"Charlotte, are you there?"

"Yes."

"So, you'll come here?"

"Okay."

Charlotte felt she was being a pushover, but she couldn't help herself. She wanted to see him. It had been over a week, a very long week, and she wanted him to see her in her new shirt. When she got to his apartment, Colin opened the door, still on the phone, saying, "Look, I can't talk about this now, I will ring you tomorrow."

He got off the phone. "Sorry about that, Charlotte. I had to take that call." He took her hand and pulled her over to the sofa and knelt down in front of her, saying, "Please accept my humble apologies," kissing her hand.

Charlotte rolled her eyes, but was pleased. She silenced that nagging voice in her head and that nagging Corinne voice outside her head, both of which were saying similar things.

Who do you think he was talking to, Charlotte? His mother?

"Corinne, stop it, I'm beginning to feel like I'm in *The Ghost and Mrs. Muir.*"

"Sorry?" said Colin.

Charlotte hadn't realized she had spoken out loud. "Nothing, I was just thinking about an old TV show I watched as a kid."

Colin looked at her more closely. "Charlotte, you are looking very fetching this evening, have I told you that yet?"

She tugged at her cardigan, which was riding upward. "I went shopping with Jodee."

"That explains it. Come over here and sit by me for a moment." She went over. He fingered the fur on her cardigan. She could hardly breathe.

He said, "I had a good time the other night."

"So did I, but that's not the reason why I came over. We really have to rehearse."

"Of course." He started kissing her neck until reading the scene was the last thing on her mind. Although they weren't rehearsing, he still called her Alma during sex, and somehow this allowed her to do things she found too bold to do as Charlotte. She made noises, felt herself lose control, things she had never done before.

❦

"Nice," said Colin, afterward, stretching out contentedly like a big cat.

"Yes," agreed Charlotte, snuggling into the warmth of his body.

"You're very uninhibited," said Colin.

Charlotte laughed. "Uninhibited? No, I'm not really, only with you."

Colin made her fried bread, which was just like it sounded, thick whole-grain bread fried in lots of butter. Served with lots of hot tea. It was delicious.

"We do have to rehearse," suggested Charlotte weakly, nibbling on her fried bread.

"There is plenty of time," said Colin.

When Charlotte got home, it was three A.M. and she opened the door to the loft as quietly as possible. The last thing she expected to see was William pacing around the room, obviously waiting for her.

"Where have you been?" he demanded.

"Out. Rehearsing, if you must know."

"I thought you were rehearsing here."

"Well, plans change."

He looked at her oddly. "Charlotte, your sweater is buttoned wrong."

She blushed and buttoned it correctly.

"Are you and Colin . . . is he your boyfriend?"

"No, we're just . . . friends, acting colleagues." She looked down at her sweater, murmuring, "Costume changes." Charlotte wondered if this was how it felt to be sixteen and be grilled by parents about your boyfriends, something that had never happened with Corinne. She hadn't had any boyfriends at sixteen and Corinne wouldn't have cared anyway. Charlotte felt like any moment she was going to be sent to her room. So much for feeling like roommates.

"Rehearsing, is that what you call it nowadays?"

"Look, I'm thirty-three years old—I can do whatever I want with whomever I choose."

"I was worried about you, Charlotte. You really should have called."

He did look worried.

"I guess I'm not used to having to check in with anyone," Charlotte snapped.

William looked hurt, and Charlotte felt guilty. She said in a softer tone, "I know you're just trying to look out for me, but I have been taking care of myself for thirty-three years. I appreciate it, but . . ."

"You're right, Charlotte. You're an adult, I should treat you like one. Now, will you think I'm being patronizing if I offer you some hot chocolate?"

"The kind with the tiny marshmallows?"

"Is there any other kind?" he replied, motioning toward the kitchen with a coffee cup.

～

It was strange, but Charlotte kind of liked him getting angry with her. A month ago, no one would have cared whether she stayed out all night.

William brought her a hot chocolate in a mug that said BAUHAUS. She sipped it cautiously, sitting down on the sofa.

"Let's have a toast," said William, carefully clinking his mug with hers. "Here's to our first fight. I think it's a good sign."

"Our first fight," echoed Charlotte, clinking her mug with his.

For those who refuse to learn by experience,
Chestnut Bud is recommended.

Chapter Twelve

THE FOLLOWING WEEK, on the night of Jodee's showcase, Charlotte arrived early to help her get ready.

"Hey, Charlotte, do you have anything for my nerves? Valium, heroin, herbs, anything? You know, this could be it, my big break. I've invited every single casting agent in the *Ross Reports*."

Charlotte gave her a swig of the kava kava she had brought with her, and then peeked out front to see if Colin was there yet. Jodee had invited everyone she knew to pack the house, and Charlotte had invited the twins, but the crowd was still looking thin.

After getting Jodee settled down, Charlotte waited on the side of the stage so she could help with the costume changes.

During the show, Jodee had twelve different outfits, each correlating to a man she had slept with. She changed her clothes and then described each man in vivid detail, from where they took her on their first date to their penis size and shape. Each date had its own music, from classical to hip hop, which played on a boom box run by Ron, who was credited on the program as producer, director and sound engineer.

Her final date was in her apartment, with Keanu Reeves movies playing on video screens all around her, as she danced to the bootleg CD of his band, Dogstar, in her underwear.

At the end of the play, there was total silence and then thunderous applause, or as thunderous a noise as twenty close friends and acquaintances and five or six total strangers can make.

Everyone swarmed around Jodee after she emerged from the curtain twenty minutes later, in a red kimono with fresh makeup.

Charlotte gave her a hug. "That was great!"

"Thanks," said Jodee, smiling beatifically at everyone, and then scowling as she surveyed the empty seats in the front of the theater where she had put her press kits, which consisted of head shots, bios and little candies.

She gathered the packages up carefully. "Those fucking casting directors. Two of them swore to me they were going to come."

Jodee's parents came up, divorced yet united in their excitement. They were beaming. "Don't worry, honey," said her father. "We made a video, we'll send it to them."

After the show, everyone decided to go to a neighborhood pub for what Jodee called her "cast of one" party.

Charlotte walked quickly to keep up with the twins.

"We loved the show," said Sophie, "although the chairs were really uncomfortable."

"Jodee's really cute. So tiny and curly," said Lauren, as if she were talking about a small dog.

The twins had noticed Colin talking to Charlotte before the show and were thrilled that he was Charlotte's scene partner. "Charlotte, don't you just love those Irish accents?" said Sophie. "It's so Liam Neeson."

Charlotte felt annoyed. "Colin is a really fine actor—he's done a lot of theater in Ireland."

"I hear they really suck in bed," said Lauren. "No pun intended."

Charlotte didn't comment, thinking about Colin and how wrong Lauren was. She didn't feel like telling the twins about her relationship with him. It was too new, too fragile for scrutiny.

"Is William here tonight?"

"No, he's working; he's been doing a lot of work at some gallery, getting it ready for a show."

"When's your mother's show at the Guggenheim, anyway? I thought that it was supposed to be soon."

"I don't know. I should find out."

They pushed open the door into the dingy space of the bar. Everyone was already standing around a large rectangular table in the back. Charlotte wanted to sit next to Colin, but everyone just sat down where they were, as if they were in a game of musical chairs and the music had stopped. Colin was at the opposite end of the table, wedged between her acting teacher and Jodee. As she looked over, he gave her a wink.

Jodee's parents had ordered chicken wings, mozzarella sticks and nachos for the whole table. They told everyone who would listen about Jodee's childhood and how they always knew that she was destined for something great.

The twins complained about the food but scarfed it down. When the waiter came over for their drink orders, the twins asked what kind of Chardonnay they were serving and the waiter looked as if he would like to strangle them. "It's vintage Soave, okay?"

"Okay, okay. Two cranberry vodkas. Do you have any Ketel One?"

The waiter shook his head and sighed. "How's Absolut?"

"Wonderful."

Charlotte ordered a vodka tonic. "Absolut is fine for me, thanks."

The twins picked at their mozzarella sticks. "Does Jodee have a thing with Colin? They seem to be very chummy," said Lauren.

Charlotte had noticed them talking but figured it was about Jodee's play. He couldn't possibly be interested in her, could he?

"No, they're just friends. She's seeing Ron."

"I'd like to be friends with him too."

Sophie confided to Charlotte that she had a yeast infection. "I've tried that Monistat stuff, but it keeps coming back, and I've been drinking Cape Codders like they are going out of style."

"Well, first of all, maybe you should stop drinking alcohol for a week, if that's possible. It's pure sugar and that may be helping out the infection. Take a bath in a little apple cider vinegar. It sounds weird, but it works. Anyway, cranberry juice is for urinary tract infections, not yeast infections."

"Thank God. I'm so sick of Cape Codders and cosmopolitans."

Ron got up and made a toast to Jodee. "Here's to the beautiful and talented star of *I slept with Keanu Reeves.*"

Everyone clapped and Jodee stood up and took an exaggerated bow.

Charlotte whispered to the twins, "He directed her."

"I'll bet," said Lauren.

"Maybe I should do a one-woman show," said Sophie. *"Infections I Have Had and the Men Who Gave Them to Me."*

Then Susan got up and said, "First of all, I want to congratulate Jodee on an original and innovative performance. And I think all of you should try to follow her example and pursue performance opportunities beyond the limits of the studio. Speaking of great opportunities, I also want to announce that I have a wonderful surprise for those of you participating in the scene study showcase. There will also be an announcement posted at the studio tomorrow, but I thought I'd give you a heads up. Our very own"—long pause—"Oscar-nominated"—long, respectful pause—"graduate of The Craft, the renowned film and stage actor E——, has graciously agreed to judge our humble scene study performance and award a prize. And . . ." Here she paused for what seemed like an eternity and glared at someone who was chomping loudly on a nacho. "The prize is going to be a small speaking role in his new movie."

As Susan sat down, everyone started clapping and talking all at once. Charlotte tried to catch Colin's eye, but he was talking to Susan with his intense I'm-an-actor look.

"I can't believe it," said Sophie.

"I know, I didn't know anything about this," said Charlotte.

"Do you think we could meet him?" asked Lauren.

"Charlotte, this means you could actually get a part in his next movie."

"I don't think so," said Charlotte, thinking that Colin deserved to get the part. It was kind of unbelievable. The scene showcase had loomed in a vague and distant way before, something she and Colin were rehearsing for but that she had never really believed was going to materialize. But now it was really happening. And she still messed up some of her lines. She would have to rehearse them over and over until they were perfect. She and Colin would have to actually begin rehearsing regularly, something they kept managing to avoid.

Sophie took out her Palm Pilot and stabbed in the date of the show with her tiny silver pen. "Now we're definitely coming to the showcase, and we expect you to win so you can introduce us to the famous actor guy."

"Hey, didn't he go out with Julia Roberts before she got married?" asked Lauren.

"Yeah, like that's going to last," said Sophie.

"I think she's the one who broke up with him," said Charlotte. "I saw something on her recently. She has serious intimacy issues. Something to do with her father."

Sophie said, "I am so not sympathetic to her."

They both looked over at Lauren, who was hitting it off with Jamal, a handsome young black actor sitting at her other side.

Sophie asked Charlotte, "What's his story?"

"Well, I always kind of thought he was, you know . . ."

"Gay?" They looked at Lauren leaning over him. "Not right now."

"Lauren believes that everyone is truly bisexual anyway."

After her third drink, Colin came over and asked Charlotte to introduce him to her friend. "This is my stepsister Sophie. And that's her twin, Lauren." She pointed over in the direction of Jamal and Lauren, who were sitting practically in each other's laps.

"Isn't he . . . ?" asked Colin.

Charlotte shrugged.

"It's so cool about E——," said Sophie.

"Yes, it'll be a great break for somebody," said Colin, subdued.

"Maybe you or Charlotte will win."

"Maybe," said Colin, as if they hadn't a hope in the world of winning.

Charlotte knew they didn't have much of a chance, the way things were going, but she was going to get better, get more focused. Colin had said she was the perfect Alma, and she was going to prove him right.

"I can't believe how many mozzarella sticks I ate. I feel sick. I'm such a pig," moaned Sophie as they spilled out of the bar onto the street.

"I gave that guy my number, what do you think?" asked Lauren.

"Sure, go for it," said Charlotte, smiling at Sophie.

Everyone stood outside the bar, saying goodbye, hugging and kissing as if they would never see each other again. Jodee gave Charlotte a little stuffed bear to thank her, then she and her parents got into a hired black limo, and she gave everyone a wave, disappearing into the night like some minor nobility. Ron the director looked longingly after the car. The twins wanted to go check out a new club they had heard about, Oblivion. The acting people started dispersing in various directions, the ones who knew Charlotte yelling out a further goodbye. The actors were always having dramatic goodbyes. Even if they were just going to get coffee, they said goodbye as if they were embarking on the *Titanic*.

Charlotte looked at Colin, wishing him toward her with every fiber of her body. And then, magically, as if he were being pulled by an invisible guide wire, he walked over to her.

"Let's go," he said, as if their departure together had already been prearranged.

The twins were staring at Charlotte, so impressed they were struck silent for once in their lives.

Charlotte followed Colin into a cab as if he were the Pied Piper and she had no will of her own. "'Bye," she yelled after the twins. "Thanks for coming."

Alone in the cab with Colin, Charlotte felt shy. Yes, they had slept together, eaten meals together, talked, rehearsed, but that didn't mean she had any idea what he was thinking about.

To fill the silence, Charlotte started talking. "Colin, from now on, I am devoting myself to learning my lines backwards and forwards. I also have some ideas for the scene. I was thinking maybe we should get some props. Not that we would do a whole set or anything, but maybe we should have a few things. For example, you could have one of those old-fashioned doctor's bags and I could have a frilly parasol."

Colin said, "Let's talk about it later."

Charlotte was quiet for the rest of the ride. She opened her pocketbook and looked at the bear Jodee had given her. The bear had a kind yet quizzical expression.

Inside his apartment, Colin checked his answering machine for messages. "Fix yourself a drink if you like, Charlotte."

Charlotte poured herself a glass of Australian wine, although she didn't think that it would mix very well with the three vodka and tonics and the chicken wings she'd had at the bar. (She had told herself they were veggie chicken wings.)

Standing across the room from Colin, for a moment she felt entirely alone, as if she couldn't even imagine them together. When he crossed the space between them and kissed her, she felt safe. But after they made love, when he stopped touching her and fell asleep, Charlotte felt the space between them widening. It was strange how alone you can feel in bed with someone you've just had sex with. Maybe she just didn't know how to be with someone, maybe she expected too much. It was so strange, she thought, sleeping next to another person, how they completely disappear into sleep, leaving you alone with your thoughts.

In the morning, Charlotte woke up with a splitting headache. It was ten o'clock. She took some arnica pills she had in her purse and went to the bathroom and washed the remaining makeup off her face. Then she went into the tiny galley kitchen and made tea—Earl Grey, putting in four sugars the way Colin liked it. She carefully walked back with the hot tea, easing slowly down on the bed, carefully putting the teacup on the floor.

"Colin," she whispered in his ear. "Colin."

She had to repeat his name louder and louder until he finally rolled over and moaned, "What the hell? What time is it?"

"Ten. Would you like some tea?"

"Thanks, luv."

That's just an expression, thought Charlotte, it doesn't mean anything.

A little later, Charlotte made toast and jam and they talked about Jodee's show.

"Mind the crumbs," said Colin, naked but very fastidiously eating his toast over a flowered china plate.

"Jodee's good, isn't she?" asked Charlotte. "I mean, she's not a great actress, but you want to watch her."

Colin gave her a strange look.

Charlotte wondered if he disagreed. "She told me after the show that a casting director had shown up incognito."

"I know. Charlotte, I need to tell you something."

He sounded so serious, she started to think it must be something serious, something medical. What could it be, a sexually transmitted disease, a brain tumor?

"What is it? Are you okay?"

Colin put his tea down and looked at her. *Intense* was the adjective that came to mind.

"I don't know how to say this to you, Charlotte, but I've asked Jodee to be in the scene showcase with me."

Why is it that people keep saying your name when they have something unpleasant to tell you. "What did you just say?"

Colin took her hand. "I really need a break, Charlotte. My visa is about to run out and I can't even get cast in a dog food commercial. I just want you to know that this isn't about us. I really care about you."

Charlotte pulled back her hand as if it were on fire. She thought she must have heard him wrong. He couldn't be saying what he was saying. "But Jodee has her own scene."

"Her partner doesn't want to work with her."

Charlotte felt frozen, like in Covington when a monster hit her with a cold spell and all her futile clicking on the mouse would only move her character forward a painful inch by inch. Colin didn't want to do the scene with her. She had a sudden bitter taste in her mouth as if she had eaten something rotten. She edged over to the far side of the bed.

"When did you ask her?"

"It doesn't matter."

She felt angry and hurt and then angry again. "It matters to me. It was last night, wasn't it, after you found out about the contest? That's when you decided to work with Jodee, isn't it?"

She could tell by the look on his face that that was exactly how it had happened. Why was he ruining everything? She loved their meetings—the rustling of the playbooks, the talks about acting, the way he looked at her.

"Charlotte, please, come here, let me explain."

She shook her head. "What's to explain? I understand. This is your career. You have to do what's best for you."

"You're angry. You have every right to be. But please, come here." Colin patted the seat next to him on the bed. He had such smooth skin, she noticed, so pale against his dark hair.

Charlotte didn't move. "Why Jodee?"

He looked embarrassed. "Well, she's had more stage experience and now she has a really good contact. Look, Charlotte, I know this acting class is just sort of a hobby for you. You have a whole other career, but this is all I have. I'm thirty-nine years old and I'm not planning on pouring drinks in some lousy bar for the rest of my life."

"I know that I'm not perfect in my lines yet, but—"

"It's nothing to do with that. Charlotte, please, come here. I want you to know I really care about you. This isn't about us."

She edged over to him slowly, cautiously. He pulled her into his arms. She still felt frozen, but enjoyed the heavy warm feel of his arms, inhaled his Colin smell. It felt strange to be comforted by the very person who was hurting you. His words kept running through her head like a script. *I really care about you. This isn't about us. Acting is just a hobby for you.* Anyway, it wasn't true. Acting wasn't just a hobby for her. She hadn't really realized it until now, but it was an integral part of her new life. Okay, maybe she wasn't going to be Meryl Streep, but Colin had told her she was good as Alma. Had he been lying? She couldn't bring herself to ask.

Colin pulled away and looked at her. "Charlotte, it's up to you. If you really want me to do the scene with you, I'll do it. I don't want this to come between us."

She shook her head, knowing that his offer to do the scene with her was a rhetorical one. He had already made up his mind.

When Charlotte got back to the loft, the answering machine was blinking insistently. She hit play and heard Jodee's voice and pressed the delete button. The twins had called, wanting to dish about Colin. Colin had called too: "Just wanted to see if you were okay. Oh, and I had a thought. Maybe you should give Jodee's old partner, Heather, a ring. Maybe you two could do that scene they were doing together and still be in the showcase. Anyway, call me." Charlotte's hand hovered over the delete button for a minute, but as much as she wanted to, she couldn't delete him.

Charlotte lay down on the bed. She felt leaden and heavy, as if she had Chronic Fatigue Syndrome. After a while, using all her strength, she edged her way under the covers. Her whole body ached. She pulled the covers up over her head, retreating into a safe warm cocoon. Except it wasn't safe. Everything had fallen apart.

She took the quizzical bear out of her pocketbook and hugged it tightly. She started crying, sobbing quietly. Charlotte hated to cry. She hardly ever cried, but when she did, it seemed to tear at something at her very center. The hurt was not unfamiliar. It was the same core of hurt she'd felt as a child, hiding under the covers during a party full of loud voices, glasses clinking, feeling like no one cared if she was alive or dead. The same core of hurt she felt when her mother got drunk and passed out, forgetting about Charlotte.

She remembered waking up once with a start during a particularly loud party, feeling like she was choking. At first the partygoers had thought it amusing to pile their coats on top of Charlotte, and she had liked the feel of the coats, all warm and soft and heavy. But after a while, she got sleepy and everyone forgot she was there. Waking with a start, panicked and suffocating, Charlotte had finally managed to push her way out from under a huge pile of coats and blankets, and ran out into the main room looking for her mother. Only after she had seen her passed out on the couch, half-finished drink still in her lap, could Charlotte go back to sleep, oddly comforted.

❦

But what was she going to do now? How was she going to face everyone at acting class? She was tempted to never go back to The Craft again, forget that this chapter of her life had ever existed. It was humiliating to admit, even to herself, that she still wanted to see Colin, but it was true. She hated him, but she still wanted to see him. How sick was that? She got out of bed slowly, feeling creaky, like a very old woman. She turned on her computer, logged on to Covington, sent a message over the server to Ix. He wasn't there. She went on-line anyway. She traveled down to the deepest, darkest tombs where the monster Gorgona lived, a hideous creature with rats for hair.

Charlotte had never defeated her. Gorgona was too strong.

In the first few weeks after her mother died, every night she would launch fireballs and arrows and live grenades at the terrible monster, but to no avail.

Charlotte would helplessly watch the life force drain out of Varlata and watch her die in a burst of flames. Then Gorgona would do a little gloating dance over her and the rats in her hair would clap their tiny paws. Charlotte's character died over and over again until Charlotte was tempted to give up and never play again.

You're addicted to that game, Charlotte. It's a good thing it isn't heroin.

Her mother's disembodied voice seemed to come from inside the computer.

Leave me alone or let me see you.

I wish I could, Charlotte, but it's just not possible.

What do you want?

I can't believe you're not going to be in the showcase—are you that much of a quitter?

What, are you spying on me now?

If I were you, I would go and kick that girl's butt.

Well, I'm not you, am I? Anyway, she did exactly what you would have done, trampled on people to get ahead. I thought you respected that.

Maybe I've changed.

Charlotte didn't respond. She got up, pressed play on the answering machine, trying to drown out the voice. Jodee had called twice more since she had been on-line.

She listened to the last message: "Charlotte, I need to talk to you, I need to know you're okay with this."

Colin had called again: "Charlotte, please call me."

There was also an e-mail from Paul. "Noticed you were in Covington. Gorgona is a tough cookie; let me know if you need my assistance."

She didn't call Jodee. Didn't call Colin, although she wanted to.

She e-mailed Paul: *I can't kill her off, she is too strong, but I am going to keep trying.*

Sweet Chestnut is the remedy for people who have reached the limits of their endurance.

Chapter Thirteen

IN THE MIDDLE of the night, Charlotte opened her eyes and remembered. She remembered that Colin was going to be doing her scene with Jodee. She remembered what an idiot she was for trusting him. She remembered that her mother was dead and was still trying to tell her what to do. She got up, drawn toward the humming of the TV like a homing pigeon.

She was wearing her flannel pajamas and pulled on a bathrobe and her pink fuzzy slippers.

William was sitting in the living room watching the small wooden-framed TV. "Sorry, Charlotte, is it too loud?"

Charlotte slumped onto the far end of the sofa, wrapping her bathrobe around her. "It's fine."

"It's 'The Women of *Melrose Place*' tonight," he said, smiling.

Charlotte didn't react and William looked at her more carefully. "Are you okay, Charlotte?"

She shrugged. "I guess."

"Do you want some tea?"

William made tea in between Heather Locklear and Courtney Thorne-Smith. She asked for Vespers, a tea made with hops, valerian and yarrow. It was supposed to calm you. She wasn't feeling calmed, however, and she couldn't focus on the TV screen. Instead of Heather Locklear, she kept seeing Colin telling her he didn't want to do the scene with her. She felt the pain in her chest again. Maybe she had tuberculosis or asthma. Or the plague. Soon she would see a dark rash, a bubo. For a while, as a teenager, she was obsessed with the plague. She imagined Colin coming to visit her in her dying moments, waving from behind a hazmat barrier.

She watched Heather Locklear talk about how she loved junk food and her relationship with Richie Sambora, how much better it was than her other relationships. Heather seemed like she would be a nice person to hang out with. Maybe Charlotte and William could invite her over for tea and cookies. Then she imagined Colin doing a love scene with Heather Locklear, kissing her.

"Charlotte, are you okay?"

It was too hard pretending to be fine. "No," she said quietly.

"Want to talk about it?"

"No."

"Okay." William sounded a little hurt, so Charlotte felt compelled to add, "It's about the play. Colin's going to do my scene with Jodee."

"Your scene. Why?"

"Well, there's this famous actor, E———, who is going to judge the competition, and the winner of the competition gets a part in his new movie. I guess Colin thinks he'd have a better chance with Jodee. She does have more experience. And she has a casting director interested in her. So Colin asked her if she would switch scene partners and work with him."

Hearing the facts out loud, Charlotte realized how creepy it sounded.

William got up from the sofa and paced back and forth. "I can't believe this, Charlotte, they shouldn't be able to do this to you."

Lisa Rinna was on TV.

"I hate her."

"Jodee?"

"No, Lisa Rinna. Or should I say, Victoria Taylor Davis McBride—that's who she was on Melrose. She's scary looking. Can you believe she named her daughter Delilah Belle?"

"Do you want me to call the school and speak to someone?"

Was this what it would have been like? For every problem, every bully who made fun of her, every grade that wasn't what she deserved, her father would have called up and fought on her behalf? It would have been nice in second grade, but it was too late now. She was thirty-three and had long had to fight her own battles.

"No, it's okay. I told him it was okay."

"It's your part, Charlotte."

"If he doesn't want to be in it with me, I'm not going to force him. He's right, I probably would forget my lines, I'm always forgetting them when we rehearse."

"I'm sure you would be fine, and anyway, that's not the point."

William brought her more tea and a shortbread cookie.

She took a bite. "This is really good," said Charlotte, licking buttery crumbs from her fingers.

"Thanks, I made it."

Charlotte nibbled on her cookie and watched the end of the Courtney Thorne-Smith segment, and for a few wonderful moments she totally forgot about Colin, but then the warm glow of the shortbread and tea started fading. "I'm going to sleep. If I don't wake up, tell the paramedics I OD'd on Dr. Stuart's Vespers tea."

"Okay, Charlotte." William gave her a little pat on her bathrobed shoulder. "Sleep tight."

His hand felt solid and heavy on her shoulder, like the paw of a friendly lion.

Charlotte slept fitfully, dreaming of Heather Locklear and Tommy Lee. In the dream, Heather Locklear had stolen Charlotte's boyfriend and Charlotte tried to scream, but no sound came out.

In the morning, her choice seemed clear. She would either have to do the other scene or never go back to the studio again.

She decided she didn't want to be a quitter.

She called Jodee's old partner, expecting a crazy woman, but Heather was actually quite nice.

"I can't believe they're screwing us over like this," she said in a throaty voice, like she had smoked a thousand cigarettes. "Jodee is good, but she's not that easy to work with," confessed Heather. "She tried to cut out all my lines and make her part into a monologue."

"Colin said you didn't want to work with her."

"I never said that. I said that she was impossible to work with, not that I wouldn't work with her."

"She's, uh, unique."

"Selfish. *Selfish* is the word you're looking for."

They arranged to meet late in the day. "We don't have much time," said Heather. "I'll fax you the script."

The scenes Heather sent her were from *Stage Door*. They were doing three short scenes from the movie version of the play. They played girls staying in a cheap rooming house who are trying to be actresses.

In the last scene, Charlotte's character goes onstage and gives a performance, moments after learning that the girl who should have had her part has killed herself. Although she was wooden as an actress before, at the end she has the emotional depth to pull it off and gives a great performance. Charlotte had never seen *Stage Door,* but she liked the script.

The lines of this play flowed much more easily than *Summer and Smoke.* Charlotte took the pages home and drilled the lines.

In the morning, Charlotte called the studio to say she was sick and couldn't make acting class.

Susan answered the phone. "Oh, I just heard that you and Colin decided to switch partners. It's kind of unusual this late in the rehearsal process, but if that's what you want . . ."

She sounded so disapproving that Charlotte was tempted to tell her the whole story. She knew Colin would get in trouble, maybe lose his job, so she said nothing except, "Yes, I'm sure, it's what I want."

"All right, Charlotte," she said with a sigh. "It's going to be a pain, but I will change the programs."

"Thank you. I appreciate it. I'll see you next week."

Jodee called again. Charlotte picked up the phone this time. "Hi, Jodee."

"Look, are you okay with this? Colin said you understood why he wanted to do it, but . . . I was wondering . . ."

Charlotte felt exhausted by the whole subject. "Jodee, it doesn't matter now."

"Are you mad? I hate it when people are mad at me. It really stresses me out. Do you want me to bring you a chocolate croissant?"

Charlotte wanted to be more angry with Jodee. She knew she

should be, but she couldn't help but be amused by someone who believed all life's problems could be solved by bribes. Unlike with Colin, she had never expected much from Jodee, so she wasn't disappointed in her. Jodee was so clearly out for herself that you knew what you were getting.

"No, that's okay."

"You still sound a little mad. Are you and Colin still . . . ?"

"No, we're not."

"I'm sorry. Are you mad at him?"

"Yes, I guess you could say that."

Charlotte went back to running over her lines. When William got home, he helped by playing Heather's character, the one played by Ginger Rogers in the movie.

☙

Charlotte went to her next acting class, getting dressed carefully, using Jodee's makeup tips: foundation, highlight, powder, blend— and most important, always use an eyelash curler.

When she walked in the room, they were already doing vocal exercises. They were all saying "unique New York" over and over again until it sounded like "nuyeek newyork." She saw Colin as she came in. He smiled at her as if nothing had ever happened. Seeing him, she felt like Miss Alma in the *Summer and Smoke* scene. She wanted to say, *Colin, you are not a gentleman.*

After class, he came over to her. He looked cautious, as if she were a wild animal and he wasn't sure if she would sniff his hand or claw him to death.

"Charlotte, did you get my messages? Why haven't you called?"

Charlotte felt suddenly on the defensive. He was standing very close to her, as if he knew that it would further weaken her resolve.

He continued, "I just wanted to thank you for doing this. I heard that you are doing the scene with Heather—I think that's great." He made it sound like she was giving money to charity.

"Heather's not a problem. She's nice. How's your scene going?" she asked.

Colin leaned in and whispered, "She's good, but she tries to improvise a little too often."

Charlotte lifted her eyebrows.

"I know I shouldn't be telling you this, but I miss talking to you."

"I have to go," said Charlotte.

He gave her a quick kiss on the cheek. "Call me."

Walking home, Charlotte tried not to miss Colin, tried not to think of them in bed together. She wasn't still interested in him, she told herself. She didn't have feelings for him—it was just sex, pure and simple.

He is quite handsome; I can understand why you were taken in. He reminds me of Eduardo, that Peruvian boyfriend I had.

This isn't about you.

Charlotte, do you think I'm not supportive enough?

Charlotte snorted. What gave you that idea?

Oh, it's just something we were talking about in a kind of seminar I'm taking.

Seminar. What seminar? Taught by whom?

I can't say, but I'd like to make amends to you.

Don't tell me you're in some kind of a twelve-step program?

It's not like that.

I know you've just realized something and want to feel better, but I'm not going to fall for that. I know all about this amends thing. It's like confession. You are absolved of all your sins, but whatever happened to me still happened. You still left me alone. You still passed out drunk and didn't give a moment's thought to me. Just because you are in some afterlife version of the Betty Ford Clinic, I'm not planning on reliving my childhood. It wasn't that fun the first time.

Ouch. Forget I asked. You're so touchy.

Do you have a sponsor?

As I said, it's not AA.

Well, do you have one?

I suppose you could call him a guide. You know, this isn't easy for me, Charlotte. Oh, by the way, thanks for The Fountainhead. *I do like to stop by my mausoleum sometimes—it's so peaceful.*

No problem.

I don't have much time for reading, though. In fact, I must run this instant or I'll be late. But Charlotte, I just want you to—I know I haven't been the best mother, but I always loved you. You know that, don't you?

Charlotte was silent.

When she was alive, her mother had promised to stop drinking so many times Charlotte couldn't count them, usually during hung-over mornings when she would get contrite and sentimental and make all sorts of promises. Once, Charlotte had made a vow to give up all candy, even her favorite Pixy Stix and Junior Mints, and Corinne had sworn up and down that she would give up drinking.

Charlotte kept her promise but found a bottle of cheap vodka in the toilet tank one day when she was opening it up to make it stop flushing. When her mother saw the bottle, she had tried to grab it from Charlotte's hand.

Charlotte had taunted her with it, running around the living room, saying, "Is this what you want? Is this what you're looking for?"

"Give it to me, you little monster, you prig."

Charlotte finally gave her mother the bottle. "Here, drink it, drink it all, I don't care what you do."

She had run back to her room and cried, wishing her father would rescue her from her mother, wondering what was taking him so long.

Charlotte walked to work. Something made her start thinking about the heart, how it was a muscle. Wasn't that a strange thought to have? A muscle. Her mother's heart was a muscle. Her mother hadn't worked out enough. Charlotte felt hysterical, like giggling. It was true, Corinne had never taken care of herself. She loved red meat, a good bottle of wine, some cheese after. Her cholesterol had probably been off the charts. Charlotte usually had cereal with soy milk for breakfast, but a block from her office, on impulse, she stopped by a French patisserie, and bought an overpriced cappuccino and a cheese Danish.

What if the heart disease her mother had was hereditary, and one day Charlotte would just be strolling along, and boom, that would be it, her underused heart muscle would shrivel up and die?

At lunch, she stopped at a health food store and bought all the remedies she would have given her mother—garlic, hawthorn berries, coenzyme Q10, and Guggul. At least her mother had something to show for her life, a body of work. What did Charlotte have? A collection of remedies, some jars of bubble bath. She didn't even have a pet.

That afternoon, Charlotte worked on a project about the side effects of antidepressants. It was ironic that some people were so unhappy with their sex lives that they took antidepressants, and then, because of the side effects of the antidepressants, they lost their libido. It was amazing how many people took antidepressants altogether. Maybe that's what she needed: a little Prozac, a little Zoloft, one potent antidepressant cocktail and she would forget all about Colin.

Tom came by and gave her a freeze-dried ice-cream sandwich. "Just what the astronauts use, lasts for a thousand years."

"Thanks," she said.

Charlotte stared at the ice cream, contemplating filing it away. The picture on the front of the package showed two astronauts floating away against a background of stars. Charlotte thought about what a disaster her life was turning out to be. If there was any time for emergency measures, it was now. She tore open the package, taking a bite of the strange-tasting futuristic ice-cream sandwich.

⁓

When she got home, she tried to call Jules in China. She got disconnected and transferred and given the runaround. She finally left a message at the adoption agency.

When Jules called her back, she sounded strange and far away.

"Where are you? I tried reaching you everywhere. What happened to the baby?"

"It didn't work out. It's complicated. I'll tell you when I get back. Anyway, enough about me, how are you?"

Charlotte wanted to ask more questions, but she could tell by Jules's tone she wasn't going to get any answers. "Nothing, it's stupid. Colin's doing my scene with Jodee."

"What? That's unbelievable. Why?"

"He thinks she can get a casting director to come see him and that he'll get cast in a movie with a famous actor."

"Not if there's any justice in the world. You still like him, don't you?"

"Yes."

"Are you still seeing him?"

"No, I don't think so."

Jules sounded sympathetic. "I'm sorry, Charlotte."

"It's okay, I'll get over it. When are you coming back?"

"After I do a trek to Kangor and Kashgar."

"Okay. Call me as soon as you're back."

"I've got to go."

Charlotte went home, stopping at a local health food store to buy some more supplies. She bought castille soap, glycerin and essential oils of peppermint, sage and ginger.

She wanted to make Jules some bubble bath to cheer her up when she got back from her trip. The loft had a bathtub, but Charlotte couldn't remember the last time she had taken a bath. It was important to have the right relaxing atmosphere for a bath and she didn't feel relaxed enough with William there.

She imagined taking a bath with Colin. They'd light candles and put on soft music. What had she done with all her time before she started thinking about Colin?

When Charlotte got home, she started making the bubble bath. The recipe was easy. Grate one bar of castille soap into a quart of warm water. Add two ounces of glycerin. The glycerin helped to make it bubble. And then add the essential oils of your choice. Today she was going to make Jules a relaxing honey-almond bath.

She added a cup of nonfat dry milk, a few drops of almond extract and half a cup of raw honey.

Charlotte filled three glass bottles with the mixture. She would give the remaining bottles to the twins. William was out and she decided to be brave and try out some of the bath mixture before she gave it to Jules. She drew a bath, as hot as she could stand it, and poured in a generous amount of the mixture. It smelled wonderful. She got out her lines to study, some seltzer, and barricaded herself in the bathroom.

The bath was so hot that it took her a while before she dared to fully submerge her body. Then she began to luxuriate in the feeling. Her body floated up under the water and she felt like some kind of mermaid.

The phone rang just as the water was becoming exactly the right temperature. Charlotte decided not to get it, but listened for the answering machine to pick up.

When she heard Colin's voice, she leapt out of the tub before she knew what she was doing. She grabbed a towel, dripping everywhere.

"Hi," she answered, trying to sound casual.

"Charlotte, are you okay? You sound weird."

"I was in the bath." Why did she tell him that?

"It was nice seeing you the other day in class."

Charlotte was silent, trying to remember to be angry with him.

"I know it's last-minute, but do you want to have dinner? I'm off tonight."

"I'm rehearsing at Heather's."

"I could meet you after. Heather's in the Village, right? I'll meet you there."

It was strange to have Colin be so accommodating. I shouldn't be doing this, thought Charlotte, agreeing to meet him at an Italian restaurant on West Third.

ఴ

They were rehearsing the scene in which Charlotte got to say the famous Katharine Hepburn line about the Calla Lilies. She was supposed to be cradling the flowers as if they were a baby. They kept rehearsing the scene, but Charlotte couldn't get the right feeling.

"Heather, would you mind if we quit a little early tonight? I have a little headache," she lied.

"No problem," said Heather. "I could use an early night myself."

"I'm never going to get this," said Charlotte, looking down at the dried flowers they were using in the scene.

"How long have you been acting, Charlotte, two minutes? Give yourself a break. You're allowed a little learning curve."

Charlotte nodded. Heather was right. It was going to take a little time.

ఴ

Charlotte met Colin at Il Mulino, an Italian restaurant so unfashionable it was fashionable. He was already waiting at a table when she arrived. When she sat down, the waiter put a tiny saucer of olive oil in front of her with tiny black olives and a chunk of Parmesan cheese swimming in it.

Colin looked at her and leaned in toward her to give her a kiss. She let him and got the same electric charge she had gotten from his touch the first time she had brushed his hand in acting class. That's just biology, she told herself, not love.

It was the first time they had ever been together that seemed like a real date. The restaurant was perfect: white candlesticks, mus-

163

sels in a spicy red sauce, homemade tortellini. Colin had osso buco.

He told her funny stories about people at his bar. She told him about Tom at the library. It was like they had just met. She could tell he wanted to talk about the scene competition, but every time the conversation veered in that direction, she steered it away. She couldn't forget that he was doing her scene with Jodee, that he would be kissing Jodee in that scene. As dessert arrived, she felt a sharp surge of anger.

"How's the scene going?" she asked abruptly.

He picked at his tiramisu warily. "It's going okay, and yours?"

"Excellent."

"Charlotte, if there had been any other way . . ."

He looked at her so sincerely, she almost believed him.

With the check, the waiters brought them tiny purple glasses of grappa that burned her throat as it went down. Colin paid, and as they walked out of the restaurant, she thanked him.

"It was my pleasure."

They stood there silently for a moment.

"Charlotte, I'd like it if you would come over."

"I can't."

He stood close and she saw an image of them having sex, his weight sinking into her.

"Can't or won't?"

"I don't know. I shouldn't be doing this."

They stood there for a few minutes, moving closer and closer to each other, until Colin hailed a cab and Charlotte slid in with him, as if she had no will of her own.

When they got to his house, he started pretending to be the lord of the manor. "Welcome to my castle," he said, in his best upper-crust accent.

Charlotte pretended she was the scullery maid. "Yes, sir."

"Come over here, you wench." Colin grabbed her.

Charlotte made faint, unconvincing protests. "But sir . . . I'm not that kind of girl, sir. Oh, sir," as he pulled her down onto his lap.

Afterward, Charlotte felt ashamed at her lack of control, her ridiculous behavior, the way she couldn't say no to Colin. She wondered why they always had to pretend to be other people with each other.

Charlotte wanted to call Jules, but she knew she wouldn't approve about Colin. Jules had come back from China babyless. She hadn't yet told Charlotte what had happened. She said she didn't want to talk about it.

Charlotte didn't know how she felt about this. She had been kind of looking forward to being an aunt, but maybe it was for the best. Charlotte remembered a little girl who had been sitting opposite her on the subway the other day, staring at her. She looked so cute and serious, it made Charlotte want to cry. The child was beautiful, but her mother looked tired, worn out, harassed. She was carrying the little girl's *Harry Potter* backpack, a Styrofoam coffee cup and her own briefcase awkwardly under one arm.

People wanted children so much, but when they had them, it was as if they had made a bargain with the devil to give up part of their life force in exchange for them.

Corinne hadn't given up much, and to her surprise, watching the mother and her child, Charlotte felt grateful. She wouldn't have wanted a mother who looked so tired, so worn out by parenthood.

Mr. Sneed called to make arrangements for the Guggenheim exhibit.

Just the thought of her mother's sculptures made Charlotte feel claustrophobic. She actually liked the loft as it was, without them. When Charlotte had moved out of Queens, she had left most of her things in storage, so the loft was still a big empty space, except for seating areas in the kitchen and in the living room. William had brought home some pieces he had found on the street, an old door and a few small tables. He was taking a class in trompe l'oeil and he had painted a garden scene on the old door and a medieval scene on some wood he had picked up on the street. "It's not the kind of painting your mother would approve of," he had told Charlotte, "but I think it looks nice."

"I can't believe the exhibit is already happening," she told Mr. Sneed.

"I know, Charlotte. As you get older, time begins to speed up in an appalling fashion. One minute you are in short pants playing with model trains, the next minute you are wearing a tie and dealing with estates and taxes." Charlotte smiled, picturing Mr. Sneed in short pants playing with a train set. "We should meet, though, and iron out the details."

"How's the gout?" asked Charlotte, changing the subject.

"Much better."

"Did you know that King Charles and dinosaurs suffered from the same affliction?"

"Well, at least I'm in good company."

*Larch is the remedy for those who feel inferior
and lack confidence in their own abilities.*

Chapter Fourteen

*C*HARLOTTE, ALL YOU really need to do is to make an appearance," insisted Mr. Sneed, who had refused to listen to any of her protests that she didn't want to be involved in Corinne's exhibit at the Guggenheim. He had left a dozen messages on her answering machine and she finally called him and arranged to meet, knowing she didn't have the heart to ignore him.

"That's all? Just an appearance?" said Charlotte skeptically, pacing around his office.

"Well, there are a few meetings and technical questions they want your input on—what your mother would have wanted, that kind of thing. Charlotte, why don't you sit down? You are making me dizzy with your pacing."

"Sorry." Charlotte sank into a brown leather armchair across from Mr. Sneed. "If I do this—and I'm not saying I'm agreeing to do anything yet—I'm not going to be available for any meetings with them. They'll have to contact me by e-mail if they have questions."

"Very well, Charlotte, as you wish. That's wonderful news. I think you'll be pleased to know that they're going to have a lovely cocktail reception with a delightful string quartet."

"Corinne would've hated that. Maybe jazz or opera, but absolutely no chamber music. She hated chamber music, she called it chamber pot music. Maybe a cellist; she did like those Bach cello suites."

Mr. Sneed tapped a pencil on his desk excitedly. "That's exactly the kind of insight they need. Let me make a note of that."

"I don't know why I'm doing this."

"Because it's the right thing to do. Can I interest you in some refreshment, Charlotte? If you like, I can attempt to make you a cappuccino on my newest addition."

Mr. Sneed paused in front of a shiny new wooden cabinet, opening the doors with a game show flourish to reveal a sleek ultramodern black Italian cappuccino machine. "A gift from a client. An Italian tile importer."

"That would be wonderful," said Charlotte. "But do you know how to use it?"

Mr. Sneed shook his head sadly. "I was hoping we could figure it out together."

After perusing the manual for a short eternity, they found the proper switches, measured out the coffee and milk and a few minutes later were rewarded by the volcanic sound of frothing milk and a slow stream of espresso.

When they were settled in with their cappuccinos, Mr. Sneed said, "Forgive me, I haven't even asked you how you are doing."

"I'm okay. Sometimes it's still hard to believe she's gone."

"I know what you mean. I may be a crazy old man, but occasionally I get the feeling that she has been here, in my office."

"I don't think you're crazy," said Charlotte, thinking, If he only knew what crazy was.

"Thank you, Charlotte. I appreciate that. And how are things with William?"

"It's okay. He's . . . it's kind of nice having someone around," Charlotte said a bit reluctantly. She didn't like to admit it, but she liked having him there. She felt safer with someone in the loft at night. She had fewer nightmares. And she felt less foolish watching old episodes of *The Mary Tyler Moore Show* at three in the morning with someone else.

"I know, I don't know what I'd do without Tristan and Isolde."

"How are they?"

"Well, Tristan seems a little listless, but maybe it's just age. Cats are so delicate." Mr. Sneed was the proud father of two snow-white long-haired Siamese cats for whom he prepared fresh tuna every night, at their own small card table.

"I'm going to make him up a nice tonic."

"That would be lovely, Charlotte."

"Did you know that William was a painter?"

"No, I didn't know that."

"He's good."

"I'm not surprised."

Mr. Sneed's phone rang and Charlotte got to her feet. "I won't keep you any longer, Mr. Sneed. Thank you for the cappuccino."

"Thank you, Charlotte, although I'm afraid I'm going to have to call you every time I have to prepare one."

"You'll be fine."

"I'll have the people from the Guggenheim call you."

"Oh, all right. Just remember, I'm not making a speech."

She kissed Mr. Sneed on the cheek and left his office, wondering what she'd gotten herself into.

I have an idea how I want to arrange the sculpture.

I was afraid of this. Charlotte was in the elevator and kept pushing the button for lobby, as if that would make her mother's voice go away.

Look, Charlotte. This show is important to me. I don't want those idiots to screw it up.

And why should I help you? You're not real.

It's a major show, Charlotte, at the Guggenheim, for god's sake, please . . .

I don't know why they'll listen to me anyway. I'm not an artist. What am I supposed to say, I'm channeling my dead mother?"

They want your input.

Yes, on whether you'd rather have caviar or pigs in a blanket. Not on the layout of the show. That's the curator's job.

Please, Charlotte.

Even now Charlotte couldn't resist her mother when she was being like this, pleading with her, needing her.

And speaking of food, I don't think they should have food and drink anywhere near my sculptures. And tell them no red wine, Charlotte, only clear beverages.

When Elena Rambeau reached Charlotte a few days later and entreated her to say a few brief words at the opening of her mother's exhibit, Charlotte demurred politely but firmly. "I'm sorry, but it's just not something I feel comfortable with."

Ms. Rambeau, however, was not to be denied, and after some polite negotiating, Charlotte agreed to be introduced, but not to say anything, just a brief *Welcome to the exhibition.*

The party was to take place on a Friday evening. The guest list was straightforward, some art mavens and beneficiaries, a few media people and whomever Charlotte wanted to invite. They gave her postcards to send out, already stamped. The postcards had a photo of one of her mother's recent pieces on it, a plaid sculpture called *Clan*. For a change, Corinne had given names to the last few sculptures she had done, instead of numbers.

Charlotte invited Colin personally. "I'd really like it if you would come," she said one morning at his apartment. They had fallen back into seeing each other with surprising ease, although not often enough for Charlotte's taste. Since the night at Il Mulino, they had played lord of the manor and scullery maid several times, as well as casting director and ingenue and Charlotte's favorite, sultan and harem slave. When she was with him, she tried to put the thought of everything else out of her mind, and almost succeeded.

"Of course, Charlotte, I wouldn't miss it for anything."

She loved lying with him after sex, just watching him, the length of his torso, the muscles and curves of his body. If she were a painter, she would paint him. She always wore an old T-shirt to bed, but he would always sleep naked, dropping his clothes by the side of the bed within easy reach, as if he anticipated having to making a sudden exit.

She would go to work late on these mornings, grateful for the fact that San Francisco was three hours behind New York.

On one rainy Thursday, she didn't arrive at work until nearly eleven. Her most regular client, Tom, was already waiting outside, standing there patiently at the door, with a *Little Mermaid* umbrella.

"It's my niece's," he said, blushing a little, indicating the umbrella, "not mine."

"Don't worry. I think it's cute. Sorry I'm so late," she mumbled, fumbling with the locks.

He was unperturbed, standing there calmly, with rain streaming over the Little Mermaid onto his shabby raincoat. "Charlotte, do you realize that New York is on a major fault line?"

"You don't say."

"Yup, it starts up near Lake Ontario and runs all the way down to Indian Point. I've decided I'm going to look into that."

"Sounds like a good idea."

Once in the building, Charlotte turned on all the lights with relief, shaking out her umbrella. She flipped the switches on all the computers and brought in the newspapers, liberating them from their wet plastic sacks.

Tom sat down contentedly in his regular spot, in front of one of the three public-use computers.

Charlotte went into her office and quickly checked her e-mail. There were three e-mails from Paul, sent only minutes ago. She hadn't really missed anything coming to work late and if she got right to work, Paul would never know. She thought of Colin lying in bed as she left him. It was definitely worth the risk.

☙

Charlotte gave Jules her bubble-bath mixture over a drink at Steak Frites.

It was so good to see her. It seemed to Charlotte that Jules had been away forever even though it had only been ten days. So much had happened in the meantime.

"You look great, Jules. I like that whole geisha look."

Jules fingered the collar of her red silk dress. "You like it? I picked it up in Hong Kong. You go to these tailors there, you pick out the fabric, give them a picture from *Vogue,* and it still costs less than anything you could buy here."

After they got their drinks and ate some french fries and Jules

172

opened her present, Charlotte asked her what had happened in China.

"I just couldn't do it," said Jules, sipping a gimlet. "I started wondering whether it was even fair to her, to that baby. No, that's a lie. I started thinking about all the things I still wanted to do: travel to New Zealand, climb Machu Picchu, sleep late—"

"Aren't you afraid of heights?"

"So what, I'll get over it. I flew all the way to China and I didn't even get to the adoption agency. Can you believe it? I was terrified. Well, at least I got an article out of it."

"I'm glad you're back. Are you sad?"

Jules looked down at her gimlet. "Yes. I don't want to feel like I'm missing out. And I still think I'd be a good mother."

"You'd be a great mother."

"I just can't do it by myself right now."

"That's okay. I was raised by a single parent, and look how well adjusted I am." Charlotte motioned the bartender for another round of drinks.

"You're fine, Charlotte. I just started wondering about my motivations. How do you even know that you are doing the right thing for the right reasons?"

"You could say that about anything. Look, just because you're not adopting that baby, it doesn't mean you are never going to have a baby."

"I guess. So tell me, what is happening at The Craft? Did you tell Colin off?"

"Not exactly."

"Oh, Charlotte." Jules had on her disapproving look. "You're still seeing him, aren't you?"

"Don't 'Oh, Charlotte' me."

"He's bad news, I just feel it."

Charlotte wanted to confide in Jules about her conflicting feelings for Colin, but every time she talked to her, she was met by such a thick wall of disapproval, she ended up defending him.

"He's treating you like crap, Charlotte, have a backbone."

"I know, but . . ."

"Sex isn't everything."

"It's not just sex, we have a connection." As she said this, Charlotte felt as if she were in a scene, trying to find the truth behind the line.

On the opening night of her mother's exhibit, Charlotte arrived early with Jules by her side for moral support. Charlotte was wearing a new, very expensive dress that Jules had talked her into. Jules was wearing a tuxedo-style jacket without a shirt underneath, which suited her curvy figure.

Standing outside the museum, Charlotte remembered a brief period when her mother insisted that she and the twins have a weekly cultural experience so they wouldn't turn into complete barbarians.

Corinne had tried to broaden their horizons with abstract art, although she despaired at Charlotte's total lack of discernment. Charlotte liked religious art, any kind of triptych or Tintoretto. The twins liked anything with celebrities, Andy Warhols or photographs, or that guy who did the poster with the woman saying, "Oops I forgot to have children."

At the Guggenheim and the Whitney and various galleries, they saw Rothkos, Pollocks, Louise Nevelsons, Louise Bourgeois, works from Fluxus, not to mention all the latest performance art and installations. Charlotte and her mother agreed on very few artists, although they both liked the quirky boxes of Joseph Cornell, which he filled with photographs or strange little objects. "Not boxes, Charlotte," her mother used to say, "*assemblage.*"

They went to all the museums, although Corinne's favorite was the Metropolitan.

"This isn't modern," complained Charlotte as she wandered around Egyptian tombs for the umpteenth time.

"Modern is a state of mind," said her mother.

The Guggenheim was also a particular favorite of Corinne's.

"Not the big toilet bowl again," the twins would groan, dragging their platform heels.

Corinne approached museums differently in different moods. Usually she would find a painting or a sculpture she loved and stand, transfixed by it, as Charlotte and the twins fidgeted behind her, not seeing whatever she saw. Or she would find a particular spot in the middle of a room and pace it out, mentally placing a piece of hers in the space and seeing how it looked. Sometimes she would speed-walk through an entire exhibit, counting the number of pieces by women artists and muttering to herself, "*Sexist bastards.*"

They all knew better than to disturb her when she was in this mood. The twins would skip ahead, giggling at any pictures with naked body parts. Charlotte would hide out in the gift shop, picking out postcards, until the twins came by to tell her how many penises and breasts they'd seen.

Now, opening the door, and seeing her mother's largest sculpture in the middle of the main floor of the Guggenheim, more prominent than Corinne herself had even imagined, Charlotte felt a strange combination of pride and sadness. The sculpture was huge, entitled *Pietà,* with one naked androgynous figure holding another in the classic Christ/Madonna pose.

Charlotte and Jules walked in slowly, silently, just taking it all in. The museum was very dark, which was flattering to the people and the sculptures. The main floor was a marvel of organized confusion. Flocks of serious girls with glasses were running to and fro with file folders and cell phones, while the catering staff was setting up the refreshments with practiced efficiency. The only people totally at ease were the waiters, who were lounging around like Siamese cats, slowly buttoning their glowing white shirts and tying their skinny black ties, catching up on theater gossip. Cases of champagne had been placed at bar stations around the room and trays of hors d'oeuvres were being set up on tables at a safe distance from the sculptures. There were tiny salmon wraps, shrimp on skewers and minuscule blinis with dots of caviar.

Besides the huge sculpture in the main rotunda, Charlotte could see there were more sculptures on the first balcony of the museum, just as Elena had told her there would be.

Charlotte was not a big fan of modern art, but she loved the shape of this museum, the way it curved around and around in a giant swirl, going up and up to the top. Charlotte had always thought of the Guggenheim like the inside of a seashell rather than a giant toilet bowl, an ocean labyrinth where something marvelous might be found just beyond one of the curving corners.

The best way to see everything in the museum was to take the elevator to the top and then circle all the way down, but Charlotte had always liked to start from the bottom and walk up, around and around, until she reached the top, like a pilgrim climbing to the top of a mountain.

As she climbed up to the first balcony, Charlotte saw that two of the smaller sculptures were from Corinne's earliest work and two from the series she had been doing when she died. The rest must still be in storage. Charlotte had insisted that they not include the sculpture Corinne had been working on when she died, although Elena had wanted to, "for authenticity."

It was strange, looking at the sculptures, some of which had loomed over her throughout her childhood, frightening, shadowy creatures that had seemed to possess immense power. They looked less formidable in the high-ceilinged room of the museum. Here, their power was contained.

Looking away from the sculptures, Charlotte glanced down at her blue silk dress with satisfaction. It suited her: a long swath of a sheath dress with tiny spaghetti straps and a square neckline. Charlotte often felt out of sync with her clothes, that they didn't represent her properly. But tonight she and her dress were one. It made her feel confident, the way the Little Princess must have felt when she put on her special velvet party dress with the sash, before her father disappeared. Charlotte wanted Colin to see her like this.

"Earth to Charlotte," she heard Jules say, having come back from chatting with the waiters holding two fragile glasses of champagne.

"What? Sorry."

"Here, drink this."

Charlotte and Jules clinked glasses and downed their champagne.

"Are we supposed to be drinking this yet?"

"You're going to need it. Oh, by the way, that Elena chick wants to see you."

Charlotte was led by one of the girls with glasses to a door that connected the round part of the museum to the square building next to it. She never knew that this little maze of offices was in here. Elena came up and grabbed Charlotte hard by the arm. "We're having a few problems. Did you see the lighting?"

"No. I didn't really notice. . . ."

"Exactly. That's what I mean. The recessed lights were a disaster, so we've had to use these new spotlights. Here, let me show you." Elena led Charlotte out of the maze of cubicles and up to the balcony. She stopped in front of a sculpture that was encased in a glow of soft yellow light.

"See?" she said accusingly. "Don't you think it's too glaring, too yellow?"

Charlotte thought it looked fine, but a voice in her ear whispered, *That's horrific, like a goddamn egg yolk. You've got to make them change the bulbs. Soft white, Charlotte. Soft white.*

"Well, it might be better with different bulbs, soft white."

"Exactly my point. We can change the bulbs. You have your mother's eye, Charlotte." Elena nodded approvingly.

Not bad, if I do say so myself.

Charlotte walked back over to Jules, who was playing with a waiter's tie. The waiter was tall and dark and looked as if he were used to having women doing things for him.

Charlotte sighed.

"I'm helping him tie it, don't give me that look," said Jules, looking over her handiwork with satisfaction. "It's not like we're having sex."

At the words "having sex," the waiter squirmed a little under Jules's ministrations.

"Jules, try to behave, okay?"

In the few minutes since Charlotte had been conferring with Elena, things had gotten more under control. The waiters were at their posts, champagne glasses were stacked in tiers, hors d'oeuvres were waiting patiently to be devoured. The lightbulbs were changed, although Charlotte didn't really see that much difference.

The twins arrived, dressed in identical skin-tight embroidered pink gowns, trailing similar dark-haired dates. They air-kissed Charlotte.

Charlotte admired their dresses.

"Badgley Mischka," whispered Sophie. "We got them at a sample sale."

"I didn't know they sold investment bankers at sample sales," said Jules.

"Ha, ha," said Lauren. "And they're not investment bankers, they're specialists."

"Derivatives," said one of the dates. "Prime brokerage," said the other, as the two of them went off to get drinks.

"Seriously, you two look great," said Jules.

"So do you," said Lauren, admiring Jules's tuxedo. "But Charlotte, you—you look amazing! That dress. Who is it?"

"I don't know, Bloomingdale's?"

"You do look elegant," said William, appearing suddenly and kissing her on the cheek. He was wearing a dark suit and looked very dapper. He came and stood by Charlotte. He approved of the soft white bulbs.

"Can you believe it? Here we are again in the giant toilet bowl," said Sophie, looking around.

"Yeah, remember our cultural afternoons? Dada blah blah," said Lauren.

"Where's Colin?" asked Sophie.

"He might be a little late."

"Well, if he doesn't show up, you should dump him," said Lauren.

"Hear, hear," said Jules.

"He'll show up," said Charlotte, more confidently than she felt.

The twins went to check out the sculptures and find their dates and the hors d'oeuvres before either of them ran out.

❦

One minute, there was no one there, just Charlotte and Jules and a gaggle of waiters. The next minute, Charlotte looked around and there were people everywhere. A small group clustered around each sculpture, but most people were hovering around the bar and the food.

"So where's Mr. Irish?" said Jules.

"His name is Colin," said Charlotte, annoyed.

"I know that." Jules looked at Charlotte and rolled her eyes. "So where is he? MIA?"

"He'll be here."

"Right."

"Don't say it. I've heard it all before: That he's not treating me well. That he shouldn't have done the scene with Jodee. That he's a jerk."

"Yes, and so what are you going to do about it?"

"Look, you don't understand, Jules. It's different for you. You've always had boyfriends. This is the first time I've ever been in a relationship that has lasted more than six weeks."

"I'm just saying—"

"I know, I deserve better."

Jules nodded. "Yes, you do."

"Look, I don't want to talk about it. I have a lot of things on my mind right about now."

"Fine," said Jules, walking away.

❦

Charlotte walked over and stood next to William. Some of the art people came over to her, looking William over curiously.

Tanya, Corinne's agent, arrived, silky scarves trailing behind her like seaweed. She kissed Charlotte on the check and held out her hand to William. "You—you look so familiar."

"Tanya, this is William. You saw him at the reading of my mother's will."

Tanya looked at William more carefully, as if he were in a lineup. "No, that's not it. I know him from before."

"I don't think so," said Charlotte.

Tanya paced around William. "Paris, 1977?"

William shook his head.

"Barcelona, '82?"

Charlotte felt exasperated. "Tanya, he used to live with my mother, before I was born."

"Right, I remember you," said Tanya, as if they were talking about last week. "You painted, didn't you?" she said accusingly.

"Yes, I did," said William, looking uncomfortable and backing up a bit, as if Tanya were a sea monster and about to swallow him whole.

"I never forget an artist. Figurative," she said, thumping him on the arm.

"Yes."

"What are you working on now?"

"Well, I'm not, really. I don't—"

Charlotte intervened. "He's doing a series of mythological scenes from a modernist perspective."

"Very interesting. Very interesting." Tanya handed him a small gold-embossed card. "Call me, we'll talk. I see great things." Tanya strode off toward her next victim.

"Charlotte, who is that woman?" asked William.

"Only one of the best art agents in New York. She could make your career."

"What career? I'm not a painter. And I haven't even done these mythological paintings yet, I was just talking about it."

"You will."

William turned the card over and over, then placed it carefully in his wallet. "Thank you, Charlotte, that was very sweet of you."

"I'm not doing you any favors. I just like the murals you've done so far."

"I know." William smiled at her. "Where's Colin?"

"Why does everyone keep asking me that?"

He changed the subject. "Are you nervous about speaking?"

"Terrified, but I'm trying to overcome my fears."

"You'll be fine, just focus on someone in the audience and picture them in their underwear."

⁕

Charlotte saw Mr. Sneed at the door and motioned him over. He was dressed in a black suit and tweed hat and had a cane with an ornate silver top.

Charlotte brought him an orange juice.

"Charlotte, this is wonderful, isn't it? Your mother would be so proud of you."

"I didn't do anything."

"That's not true. Elena told me what a help you were with setting this up. You did the right thing, Charlotte."

"How's the cappuccino machine?"

"A temperamental monster. You'll have to come over and sort it out."

"What are they going to do with the sculptures after this?"

"As I understand it, they'll keep some in the permanent collection and then lend some out for other exhibits."

"Do you think they might lend me one?"

"Of course, Charlotte, I'll speak to Elena about it."

"Thanks. I just think the loft needs one—a small one."

"Any particular one you had in mind?"

"There was one I used to play under when I was little, I think it's called No. 16A. It looks sort of like the Eiffel Tower."

Colin hadn't arrived yet and it was already time for Charlotte to give her introduction. Elena called her up to a makeshift podium in front of the champagne. She introduced her as Corinne's beloved daughter, Charlotte, described her and Corinne as a team that roamed the world, a kind of mother and daughter Thelma and Louise, fearless, impoverished, creative.

Before she spoke, Charlotte looked out at everyone. She looked at Jules and envisioned her underwear. Jules was partial to day-of-the-week bikini underwear she got at Kmart, especially the Thursdays. The waiter guy would probably have some stylish boxers, paisley in a silky fabric. Elena would have bloomers, long old-fashioned antique bloomers. Charlotte looked around the room and tried to make eye contact like they taught in acting class, taking one last long sweeping look for Colin, who was nowhere to be seen and sometimes didn't wear underwear at all.

She took a deep breath and began. "I want to thank you all for coming. It was always my mother's great dream to exhibit at the Guggenheim and I know she would have been thrilled by this exhibit and by your support." It was true. Corinne would have loved it. And she wasn't here. Charlotte felt her throat start to close up, and looked out into the crowd again. She saw the twins in their tiny Cosabella thongs and Tanya in a pair of men's boxers. She continued, "I want to thank the Guggenheim and especially Elena Rambeau, who has done such a wonderful job with my mother's sculptures." Looking at Elena, Charlotte revised her underwear appraisal and decided she would wear antique silk underwear she picked out in French flea markets. "And I'd also like to thank all the behind-the-scenes people, who have made this evening so special. Thank you."

There was silence until everyone realized she wasn't saying any more, and then people started to clap. Next, a well-known critic got up and spoke monotonously about the artistic significance of the work.

The twins came up to her afterward. "You looked so dignified up there, Charlotte, so elegant," said Sophie.

ᙬ

Charlotte expected her mother to have more comments, but there was absolute silence on that front. Well, she got what she wanted, thought Charlotte, so she's probably having a big old margarita, wherever she is.

"She would have liked this," said William, looking nostalgically into his wineglass.

"She would have, wouldn't she?"

"Charlotte, I'm so glad you invited me."

"No problem. I'm glad you came."

"Charlotte, can you believe we have been living in the loft for almost six months together?"

Charlotte didn't believe it either, actually. "Soon you'll be able to move out," she said.

"I guess so. You too."

As William said that, Charlotte realized that she didn't really want to move, not yet, that she wanted to stay in the loft, keep watching *Buffy* and "true Hollywood" specials. There had been too many disruptions this year already.

"Have you thought about what you're going to do after the year is up?" William asked.

Charlotte felt a rush of sheer panic. "No, not really."

"You know, Charlotte, we don't have to sell the loft right away. We could stay there, split the expenses, build a few more walls if we have to."

"Not forever."

"No, just till we figure out our next step."

ꞓꞔ

The twins came up and started talking to Charlotte and William.

"Hey, Charlotte, there's your boyfriend," said Lauren.

Colin strolled in, wearing black jeans and a LEMONHEADS T-shirt. His concession to formality was a black leather jacket, a little less scruffy than his usual one.

He came over to Charlotte and kissed her. "Sorry I'm late, I had an audition."

"I thought it was in the morning."

"No, they changed the time."

Charlotte decided to believe him. She introduced him to everyone and he shook their hands and looked each of them in the eye, his charm turned on full blast.

"You missed Charlotte's speech," said Sophie.

"How did it go?"

"She did fine. Did you get the part?" asked William.

"It's just a one-liner in a movie. I'd be the white waiter."

"The what?" said Lauren

"Well, everyone else in the movie is black, and I'm the waiter."

"That's kind of funny." William chuckled, repeating it to himself. "The white waiter."

Charlotte stood next to Colin, feeling that she could breathe for the first time all evening. He had come through. He was standing beside her—her person. She was part of a couple.

"Your friend doesn't like me," whispered Colin, alluding to Jules's glaring at him from a distance.

"She's very loyal. But once she gets to know you, she'll like you," said Charlotte halfheartedly, knowing that Jules would never like Colin.

"Any chance of having a bit of that champagne?"

Charlotte motioned to Jules's waiter, who seemed to be glaring at Colin too but handed them two glasses.

They clinked glasses. "Here's to your mum."

Colin downed his like a shot, grabbing another from the tray of the departing waiter.

❦

In the bathroom, Charlotte and Jules fixed their makeup.

Jules said, "I checked: no hereditary diseases, no mental illness. They all died peacefully in their sleep."

"What the hell are you talking about?"

"Joel, the waiter."

"Oh."

"Possible father material," said Jules, gesturing at her stomach with a mascara wand.

"Right."

"I guess Colin's not so bad," conceded Jules, brushing imaginary lint off her tuxedo jacket.

"You don't mean that."

"True, but I'm trying."

Colin was behaving. He shook hands with everyone, bonded with the dates of the twins and even managed to get Jules to speak a few words with him about Ireland.

William said to Charlotte, "I guess he's okay. We should have him over for dinner sometime." It was strange to hear William use the word *we*.

The opening was only supposed to last till nine and at about nine-thirty everyone left en masse. Elena came out and declared the exhibit to be a smashing success and vaguely said in Charlotte's direction that she would be in touch. There were air kisses all around and crushing hugs from Tanya.

William and Mr. Sneed shared a cab, but everyone else went to a fancy Mexican place in Tribeca afterward and did shots of tequila, which was Colin's idea. The twins got into it and Jules even had two shots, refusing to be seen as a wimp.

After two shots, though, everyone but Colin had had enough.

"You guys are wimps, you Americans," said Colin, downing his third shot.

"At least our bars don't close at midnight," said Jules, leaning on the shoulder of Joel the waiter.

The investment bankers said they were in training and only drank beers.

Colin kissed Charlotte, a hostile, sloppy tequila kiss.

When they got back to Colin's apartment, Charlotte had a flicker of hope that some romance would be salvaged, despite it all. Inside the apartment, Colin grabbed her and pressed her against the door, and she tried to forget about everything: how he had been so late, so underdressed, so unreliable. She tried to be in the moment, tried to recapture that feeling she'd had the first time she came over to his apartment, that she was so lucky to be with him—and was succeeding for a second, until she felt his dead weight collapsing against her and realized that he was falling asleep.

Unbelievable. She shook him. "Colin, go lie down. I'll bring you some aspirin." Charlotte usually didn't like to use aspirin, but this qualified as an emergency and she didn't have any arnica to give him.

He walked over to the bed, denying being drunk, denying being tired, denying having been asleep. "I don't want any of your bloody aspirin. Or any of your witch remedies. What I need is a drink." He lay down on the bed and passed out before he could take the aspirin or argue about it.

Charlotte looked at Colin and felt the same revulsion she used to feel when her mother got drunk. He was lying there without a care in the world, certainly none for her, and she felt alone, utterly and totally alone.

Charlotte had a sudden, sharp longing for her mother. She wished she could be a little girl again on one of those nights when Corinne would read *The Fountainhead* to her. She wanted to feel her physical presence, smell her Shalimar, hear the words she didn't really understand, know that she wasn't alone.

But she was alone. Her mother was gone. That was just a fact of her life now. People were always complaining about their mothers, but Charlotte would never again have that luxury. She took off her dress, put on an old shirt of Colin's and swallowed his aspirin. She tried to fit herself into the bed, but Colin was splayed diagonally across it and no matter how much she pushed him, he wouldn't budge.

Chapter Fifteen

ILLIAM HAD BEEN working more and Charlotte was rehearsing almost every night, so their brief interlude of carefree late-night television watching had been put on hold.

The last time they had watched *Buffy* reruns, Buffy and the cute blond vampire, Spike, were having a thing and William had used it as a leaping-off point to discuss Colin and his unsuitability.

During the commercial, he had muted the TV in a purposeful way. "Charlotte, I really think what Colin did to you was inexcusable."

She stared at a commercial for Nike sneakers, all the people running and jumping on screen making her feel weary. "If I've forgiven him, I don't see the problem."

"That *is* the problem. How can you forgive him for throwing you over like that?"

Charlotte felt compelled to defend Colin. "Look, it wasn't such a big deal. Acting is just a hobby for me, anyway. I like it, but it's not my dream."

"What is your dream?" asked William.

"I don't know—I guess I'd like to do something with healing."

"Well, even if it isn't your dream, what he did isn't right."

"If he has a better chance with Jodee, then he should take it." Charlotte found herself believing the words as she was saying them.

"But it's your scene, you worked hard on that."

"Look, it's over. Ancient history. I don't want to argue about this."

Back in her room, Charlotte had seethed. Who was he to tell her anything? At least her mother had been around in her half-assed way during Charlotte's childhood. William had never been there for her. He had left her mother, not even knowing she was pregnant, and now here he was, trying to tell her what to feel about Colin. But the worst thing was that she knew William was right. Colin shouldn't have switched scene partners. It was her scene. She was supposed to be Alma. She had worked so hard on her character, dried wildflowers between the pages of old books, worn that stupid Alma dress.

A week after the opening at the Guggenheim, Jules dragged Charlotte to one of her yoga classes.

"I really don't have time for this," protested Charlotte.

"Look, you need to relax, we'll just go to the basic class. It'll be good for you."

Charlotte agreed because she hardly ever got to see Jules anymore. Charlotte and Heather were rehearsing furiously every other night, determined not to make fools of themselves in front of the famous actor, determined to show Colin and Jodee that they were capable of doing good work.

For so long, her life had been so predictable, so calm, and now it seemed like everything was happening at once.

Paul had even e-mailed her and said he might be coming in to town for a conference and asked her if she wanted to have dinner with him. Charlotte felt nervous at the thought of meeting him face-to-face, but was excited at the same time. She hoped they could be real friends, not just employer and employee. She also hoped he wasn't coming to fire her, because she couldn't take that right now.

The yoga studio was down on Thirteenth Street. During the downward dog pose, Charlotte copied the instructor and put her hands and feet on the floor and her butt in the air, but she started to feel like she couldn't breathe. The instructor told them to focus on their breathing, but whenever Charlotte did, she started to think about the environment and the depletion of the ozone layer.

Tom believed that global warming was already in a very advanced stage, and that big business was hiding the evidence. What if he was right and gradually, imperceptibly, the air was becoming unsafe?

Luckily, the instructor told them to come out of the pose at that moment.

There was a man on the mat next to Charlotte who kept making heavy breathing noises during the whole class. Every time Charlotte had ever taken a yoga class, there was always a man like that. It was as if men felt emasculated by yoga and they could only counteract this by snorting and breathing as if they were lifting weights at Gold's Gym throughout the poses.

Charlotte knew you were supposed to be compassionate in yoga, but she couldn't help feeling annoyed by a woman who kept walking back and forth during the class wearing low-slung parachute pants with a thong sticking out. At first Charlotte thought it might have been inadvertent, until she saw the woman purposefully pull down her pants so her thong would be visible. The charm of thongs eluded Charlotte, who felt they were distinctly unsanitary.

During the corpse pose, Charlotte dutifully lay down on her back with her palms facing upward and tried to become attuned to cosmic energy until the heavy breather on the mat next to her actually started snoring. Out of the corner of her eye, Charlotte saw the teacher walk over and gently nudge him until he stopped.

Not that Charlotte was actually relaxing anyway. Thoughts were racing through her mind like jumping beans. Lines from the play. She thought about Paul—hoped she would have enough time to see him.

Mostly, though, her thoughts were centered on Colin. Half the thoughts were that she should never call him again, that he was a jerk; the other half were going over scenes of them together in her head, wanting to see him again.

Then, for a moment, everything left her mind, leaving her with a wonderful blankness.

The instructor rang a tiny silver bell, and for a moment Charlotte had to struggle back to consciousness and remember where she was. They om'd a few times and repeated the closing chants, sitting cross-legged on their multicolored Indian blankets. Charlotte liked the ending chant:

> *Lead us from unreal to real,*
> *lead us from darkness to light.*
> *Lead us from the fear of death to the*
> *knowledge of immortality.*
> *Let the entire universe be filled with peace and joy,*

love and light.
Bow to that light.

Then everyone pressed their palms together in front of their chests and bowed, saying, "Namaste," which was like thank you.

※

"That was great. You look so relaxed, Charlotte," said Jules as they were changing in the cramped dressing room.

"I do?" asked Charlotte. "Hey, Jules, do you ever feel weird when you are in corpse pose?"

"You mean Savasana?" said Jules, who insisted on using the proper Sanscrit names. "Weird how?"

"Like you can't breathe."

Jules laughed. "You are the only person who would feel anxious during the most relaxing pose in all of yoga."

"So, I guess that's a no."

※

Afterwards they went to Tea and Sympathy, a tiny tea shop nearby, for scones and Earl Grey tea served in quirky teapots. Charlotte's had an Alice in Wonderland pattern, while Jules's was shaped like a tiny castle.

Jules got a Welsh rarebit, or *rabbit,* as the waitress called it in her harsh Cockney accent.

"Your mother's show was really good," said Jules, between cheesy bites. "I had such a hangover, though. Remind me never ever to drink tequila again."

"I know, it was brutal. How's Joel the waiter?" asked Charlotte. "He was pretty cute."

"Didn't work out. Musician. I did meet someone new, though."

"Really?"

"Yeah, it's this guy in my Bikram yoga class. They make the room really hot and I had forgotten to bring enough water and he gave me some of his Smartwater."

"You have to let me meet him."

They ordered more tea, and Jules asked, "How's Colin?" in the way one asks about a relative in a mental institution or a wayward child.

"Great. We've been seeing a lot of each other." This wasn't quite true. Their dates had actually become much more infrequent. To be honest, since the Guggenheim opening, there had only been one time, late at night, at his place.

Jules finished her Welsh rarebit, looking skeptical.

"It's true, things are good. Anyway, I thought you said at the opening that he wasn't so bad."

"Well, he's not the Antichrist, but he doesn't treat you that well. Everything seems to be at his convenience, like the way he was late to your mother's show."

"It wasn't his fault. He had an audition."

Charlotte tried to sound indignant, but deep down she wondered if Colin really had been at an audition that night. She couldn't admit it to Jules, but she thought it was strange that he had never mentioned it again.

"He just doesn't seem to make you happy."

"I am happy. And it's not like your relationships are so perfect."

"Don't turn this around to me. We're talking about you and Colin."

"I'm just sick of everyone telling me they know what's best for me."

"Fine, let's drop it," said Jules in a flat hard voice. Charlotte could tell she was mad. She didn't get angry often, but when she did, Charlotte knew from experience it stuck.

"You're mad now."

"No, I'm not." Jules motioned to the waitress for the check.

"So, do you want to get together next week? More yoga?"

"Actually, I'm going to be out of town—I have an assignment."

"Oh."

They left awkwardly, in separate directions, like people who hardly knew each other. Charlotte felt angry too. On some level, she knew Jules was right about Colin, but she didn't want to hear it. She was finally in a relationship, finally enjoying herself, and no matter what her doubts were, she wasn't going to let anyone ruin it for her.

When she got back to the loft, there was a message from Heather, canceling rehearsal because she had a date.

"Who is it?" asked Charlotte, calling her back. "Someone from the studio?"

"You don't know her," said Heather.

"Her?" said Charlotte, confused for a moment.

"You didn't know?"

"Well, you seemed to be so sympathetic about Colin and know a lot about men."

"Believe me, I've gone out with enough people, men and women, to know the type."

"So, who is she?"

"Not an actress."

"That's great. Have fun!"

Charlotte tried to call Colin, but there was no answer. She didn't leave a message.

William was out and even her mother had gone silent. Charlotte didn't care. She just wanted to know one way or another if Corinne was really gone for good. Okay, maybe she cared just a little. You just start getting used to people, and they disappear.

Charlotte put on some music. She picked out one of William's CDs, Johnny Cash, sad and tragic, perfect for her mood.

She lay on her bed in a kind of corpse pose, angry with Jules and with William, wondering why they called it corpse pose anyway. It is not relaxing to think of yourself as a corpse.

She got up and decided to take a bath so she'd be ready to go out in case Colin called. While she was in the bath, she began to have a glimmer of an idea about killing Gorgona. Her strategy wasn't clear yet, but it had something to do with ice. Looking back, she realized how Gorgona always used fire to kill her: walls of fire, bolts of fiery lava, raging flames. Varlata had returned fire with fire, trying to kill her with lightning and fire-tipped arrows and live grenades, which had done little or no damage. When you were playing the game, you tended to use the same kind of weapons until you developed a killing proficiency in them. Varlata had never used ice weapons because she would have to start at the bottom level with them, but maybe now she could get the smith to make her some kind of special ice-tipped arrow or get Ix to work a deep-freezing spell. Luckily, in her town strongbox she had plenty of gold to pay for it.

Charlotte had made a special relaxing bath for herself, putting a few drops of Rescue Remedy into the basic bubble-bath mixture. It didn't have any smell, but she thought it would help her remain calm. And she needed to be calm as she waited for Colin to call.

She had confessed to Heather at their last rehearsal that she was still seeing Colin. Heather didn't seem surprised. She had taken a long drag on one of her Marlboro Lights and shrugged eloquently. "Hey, I know how it is—cute straight men are like needles in a haystack." A few minutes later, she had turned to Charlotte and said, "You know you could do better."

"Et tu, Brutus?"

Heather had laughed. "Well, it's true."

Everyone was saying this kind of thing to Charlotte lately. It only made her want to see Colin more, as if they were star-crossed lovers forbidden by their families to meet.

Did the others think it was so easy to meet men? Before Colin, the last three guys she went out with were blind dates. One was an accountant who sent back his food every time they went out to dinner. He seemed to be convinced that the restaurant was hiding the special good food in the back and that he was getting the dregs.

"I want the white-meat chicken. You know," he would say confidentially, "the stuff you keep in the back, not this old chicken you give to everybody."

The waiters looked at him with thinly disguised scorn, as if he were a recent release from a mental hospital. "Sure, sure, we'll bring you the good stuff."

After each of their three meals together, he spent ten minutes complaining. He complained about the food, about the service, about the exorbitant prices.

They never slept together, although he was always trying to lure her back to his house in Great Neck. She did go over to his house once, where all the furnishings were from the early sixties, down to the green shag rug and the Plexiglas coffee table. He was still living in his parents' house, and even after they had retired and moved to Florida he had never seen the need to change anything.

"Isn't it great?" he had asked Charlotte, opening up the huge bar cabinet and offering her a vermouth.

"Great," she had told him, wishing she were anywhere else.

For months afterward, she would get hang-ups on her machine and she knew it was him.

Charlotte was glad that Colin still wanted to see her, even though it had become increasingly infrequent. He was beautiful, talented and they had wonderful sex. Okay, he was a little selfish, a little unreliable, but you can't have everything you want, can you?

Charlotte, you are going to shrivel up like a prune if you don't get out of that bathtub soon.

Charlotte pushed some bubbles over her nakedness. "Corinne, get out of here. Could I have a little privacy, please?"

I'm your mother, it's nothing to me.

You're unbelievable.

I'm just trying to help you.

Don't bother.

They're right, you know.

What? Who?

About Colin. Your friends. Your father. They don't trust him. Neither do I.

It's none of their business, or yours.

He hasn't called, has he?

He will.

I know you don't trust my advice.

That's an understatement.

But Colin's not for you. He doesn't love you.

Charlotte was close to tears. Thanks a lot.

Charlotte, I'm not trying to hurt you, I'm trying to protect you.

Protect me, that's a good one. Anyway, you're wrong. He does care about me. Why should I listen to you anyway? So I can end up alone at fifty-five, drinking myself into a stupor every night and sleeping with art students who are hoping for a contact with a gallery owner?

That hurt, Charlotte.

Good, what happened to you being supportive anyway?

I'm a work in progress.

The phone rang and Charlotte could feel her mother's presence melt away.

*

It was Colin. He wanted her to come over around midnight.

She went, fueled by her mother's disapproval. They ate sesame noodles and vegetable dumplings and shrimp toast.

"You can't get this kind of take-away in Ireland," said Colin, scraping the last sesame noodle out of the cardboard container with satisfaction.

Charlotte was always trying to draw Colin into talking about his childhood, but he never really said much.

He said how he'd like to take her to see some of the countryside. "It's beautiful, Charlotte, I know you'd love it."

The phone rang. He didn't answer it, deftly turning down the ringer volume with one hand and pulling her toward him with the other. "I don't want to be disturbed," he said, kissing her neck. "I want to give you my full attention."

She thought it was kind of romantic but couldn't help asking, "Don't you want to know who it is?"

"I'm sure it's nobody," he said, kissing her neck.

*

In the morning, she got ready to go to work, taking a shower in his minimal-hot-water shower.

When Colin was in the shower, she listened to the message on the machine, but it was only a hang-up. She carefully reset the volume button.

When she left in the morning, he didn't say anything about seeing her. That was typical. He would call her at nine or ten at night, but he would never make plans to get together ahead of time. Occasionally she would try to suggest something or ask him what he was doing later, but he would just say, "We'll see."

He just didn't like to plan ahead, she told herself, walking down his street, that's understandable.

✿

A few nights later, Charlotte was taking a bath and she heard William's voice in the apartment. He wasn't alone. She heard his voice and then a high tinkling laugh that followed him.

"Charlotte," he called out.

"I'm in the bath," she answered.

"I'm here with my friend Zoe," he called out loudly.

As she quickly pulled out the plug on her bath, Charlotte tried to imagine what a Zoe would look like. Probably a tall, willowy blond, probably too young for him. She got out of the bathtub. She couldn't relax with a Zoe in the apartment. She quickly toweled off, grateful that she had brought her clothes into the bathroom with her.

"Hi," she said in their general direction as she emerged damp and dressed from the bathroom.

Zoe was not as she had imagined. She wasn't tall, blond and willowy. Worse, she was close to William's age, with long dark hair and a sympathetic expression.

Charlotte hated her on sight.

"Zoe and I are in a Tuscan cooking class together."

"I've heard so much about you, Charlotte," said Zoe, smiling like a psychotherapist.

"Oh, have you?" said Charlotte dryly.

"Yes, your father has been telling me all about your interest in alternative medicine and how you are taking acting classes. I think it's wonderful."

"Thanks," said Charlotte, knowing she was expected to say more, engage the newcomer in polite conversation, but she just stood there and eventually an uncomfortable silence drifted over the three of them. *I hope she's not going to sleep over*, thought Charlotte, feeling like a sullen teenager.

William broke the silence. "Well, I guess we should get going. I just wanted to show Zoe the loft and some of my paintings."

With Charlotte's permission, William had begun painting scenes on one of the walls of the loft. He had started a series from Greek mythology, beginning with Orpheus descending, then Artemis and Orion. Now he was working on Cupid and Psyche.

Charlotte had let him do it, thinking she could always have the wall repainted if she didn't like it. But she did like it. She loved the paintings, but now, as she stood there admiring them with Zoe and William, she started to feel as if the scenes were taking over the apartment, and that Artemis was mocking her.

William turned to her. "Charlotte, we're going to that little Italian place on Prince. We'd love it if you would join us."

"I can't, I'm seeing Colin later."

William frowned as he buttoned up his jacket. "All right, I'll see you later."

Zoe tugged on a poncho and they were out the door.

It wasn't true. Colin hadn't called in days, but she just wanted to punish William. And maybe saying it would make it come true.

Charlotte paced around the apartment. She didn't know what to do with herself. Not that she didn't have things to do. She could rehearse her lines again, try to fix the bubble-bath mixture so it made more bubbles.

Instead, she did what she usually did when she was anxious: went on-line and tried to kill Gorgona, this time with an ice-tipped arrow. But the arrow melted into nothingness and Varlata was killed effortlessly by Gorgona with a wave of a fiery hand. Charlotte signed off in frustration.

Why wasn't he calling her? Why had she let him in her life again?

She pictured William and Zoe, their heads bent over a Chianti bottle candle, sipping rough red wine and twisting spaghetti strands around their forks.

Everyone was paired up. The twins were dating twins they had met on-line. William had Zoe. Heather was dating the nonactress girl and Jules, well, who knew what Jules was doing, but she probably wasn't doing it alone. She hadn't talked to Jules since they'd argued after yoga class. Charlotte had picked up the phone to call her several times, then put it down.

Charlotte went to the refrigerator, searching its barren depths for something to distract her. She saw the beers she had bought for Colin huddled in the back of the refrigerator, calling to her. Neither she nor William had done any shopping in a while, so there was no food—no real food anyway. She opened a can of Guinness and drank it straight from the can, the bitter chocolately liquid sliding down her throat. What was it they said? *Guinness is good for you.*

When William came home, Charlotte was huddled on the couch, half asleep, watching *Stage Door*, feeling inadequate to Katharine Hepburn.

He came over to her, concerned. "Charlotte, are you okay?"

"It's just so sad."

"What is?"

"She died."

"Who?"

Charlotte pointed to the screen. "Kaye died," said Charlotte, wiping her eyes with her sleeve. "The good actress. Katharine Hepburn will never be as good as Kaye. And I will never be as good as Katharine Hepburn."

William looked confused. He surveyed the array of empty Guinness cans on the coffee table. "Was Colin here?" he asked, as if Colin must have been the real reason for making Charlotte upset.

Charlotte wanted to tell him about Colin and how he hadn't called and how she was afraid he had gotten tired of her and how scared she was to do the play, how worthless she felt, but she managed to keep it together, keep her breath steady, stop crying and stare at the TV screen.

"So what did you think of Zoe?"

"She seems nice," said Charlotte carefully.

"I'm very glad you liked her. Don't stay up too late."

He could have stayed to talk to her. He probably wanted to go to sleep and dream of Zoe.

He didn't want to hear about her stupid problems anyway.

She drank the flat dregs of Guinness and watched the very end of the movie, when Katharine Hepburn is able to say her lines with feeling because her friend has died. Charlotte cried harder, feeling sad, small and alone.

There's something so sad about seeing the credits to a movie roll by, thought Charlotte, so final. She wondered where her mother was when she needed her, why even that disembodied voice had deserted her.

Paul called the next morning. Charlotte was hungover and barely recognized his voice.

"Charlotte, I just wanted to let you know that I am going to be in town on Thursday, so I was still hoping we could get together. What does your schedule look like?"

Charlotte was taken aback. She wanted to see Paul, but all she could think about was Colin.

He mentioned a time and she said, "Sure, that would be fine. Do you want to come by the office?"

Charlotte met Heather for a lunch rehearsal. They knew their lines by heart but were still working out a few kinks in their scene.

Charlotte still didn't feel *in the moment* when she was saying her lines.

Heather was philosophical about it. "I can't believe it's next week, Charlotte, but I think we're as ready as we'll ever be."

"I'm trying not to think about going up on an actual stage in front of actual people."

"They're not actual people, they're actors. But we could do a dress rehearsal with our costumes," suggested Heather.

"Okay, we can do it at my house. Why don't you come over tomorrow night?"

"And break the rule about no home rehearsals?"

"Believe me, it's already been broken," sighed Charlotte.

"I'll bet. It would be interesting to see how we do in front of an audience."

"I'll see who I can round up."

Chicory is the flower remedy recommended
for misdirected love energies.

Chapter Sixteen

CHARLOTTE WORE A blue shirtwaist dress for the rehearsal and combed her hair to one side to make it look longer and more old-fashioned.

Charlotte and Heather got dressed in her bedroom. They were nervous, even though they only had an audience consisting of William and Zoe and the twins, who were sitting in front of a makeshift stage area in the living room.

They walked out and Charlotte said her lines and Heather said her lines, but it all seemed flat, with none of the feeling of the movie.

At the end, no one clapped.

"That's it," said Heather. "Finito. End of scene," promoting a flurry of clapping among the twins and William and Zoe.

"You know what they say, 'Bad dress rehearsal, good show,'" said Heather gamely.

"And never say *Macbeth* in a theater. You have to call it 'the

Scottish play.' Otherwise it's really bad luck," said Charlotte, relieved their performance was over.

"Is that true?" said Lauren.

"Totally," said Sophie.

€€

They had a makeshift supper after the dress rehearsal. There was leftover Chinese food, the twins had brought mini-muffins and Charlotte had contributed snacks of soy crisps and Smart Puffs. Heather had brought some Krispy Kreme doughnuts and Zoe and William had made vegetarian lasagna and salad.

"This is delicious," said Sophia, scarfing down a second helping of lasagna.

"Yeah, what's in it?" asked Lauren through a mouthful of food.

"Spinach, portobello mushrooms, goat cheese," said William. "It's from our cooking class." William and Zoe looked at each other, admiring their creation.

€€

Charlotte had never had people over when she lived in Astoria, but here it was actually fun. Certain spaces make people behave a certain way. Her old apartment, with its shabby carpeting and low ceilings, made people feel deprived; the loft, with its odd shapes and large windows, made people feel relaxed and expansive.

Heather was walking around with a glass of red wine in her hand. "Great space. I like the way it's so open. What's all this?" she asked, pointing to Charlotte's shelf full of mixing equipment, glass jars and tiny eyedroppers.

"Oh, that's for my homeopathic remedies. I make them. It's kind of a hobby."

"Yeah, any health problem you have, Charlotte can fix," said Lauren.

"Actually, I do have some back problems."

Everyone looked at Charlotte expectantly.

"Arnica and Traumeel. Traumeel is this great homeopathic cream for injuries. I have some—I'll give it to you before you leave."

"Thanks, Nurse Charlotte."

Everyone admired William's latest work, a mural he had drawn on a large piece of wood in the living room.

"Isn't it great?" said Zoe.

"Cupid and Pysche, right?" said Heather. "I used to love Greek mythology—I had this book I would read over and over."

"I had a mythology book too," said Charlotte.

"Psyche sort of looks like you, Charlotte," said Sophie, staring closely at the painting.

"No, she doesn't," said Charlotte.

"Maybe just around the eyes," offered Heather.

William came up and examined his work as if he hadn't seen it before. "You know, you're right, there is a likeness."

"The unconscious is powerful," said Zoe.

Heather plopped down on the sofa and lit a cigarette.

Charlotte handed her an ashtray. Zoe coughed pointedly, but Heather ignored her. William opened a window and let in a blast of cold air.

"I've always wanted to write a remake of Cupid and Psyche. A play," said Heather. "I thought I could make Psyche a psychologist."

"And Cupid could run a dating service," said Charlotte.

"We should do that, write a play together—and then star in it," suggested Heather, taking a drag from her cigarette.

"Let's just try to get through this performance," said Charlotte.

"I can't believe the showcase is next Friday," said Lauren.

"Neither can we," said Heather. "Well, at least we know our lines."

"You were good," said Charlotte. "I was terrible."

"We were both pretty bad," said Heather.

"You'll be fine," said William. "We're looking forward to it." He put his arm around Zoe and beamed at Charlotte like a proud father. Even if he didn't feel like her father, it was still nice to have the support.

"Especially to seeing E——," said Lauren, putting on lip gloss, as if he might show up at any moment.

༄

The twins rushed out to meet their dates and Zoe and William left to see a late movie about the Holocaust.

"Those two seem very happy," said Heather as she and Charlotte were clearing off the table.

"They do, don't they? And how was your date?"

Heather looked shy, for once. "It was good."

"You're going to see her again?"

Heather nodded, smiling to herself. "Yeah, I think I am. And how about you? How's our favorite teacher's assistant?"

Charlotte concentrated on scrubbing the lasagna pot. "I haven't seen him lately."

"He'll turn up. I told you. I know the type."

Heather was right. A couple days later, just as Charlotte was finishing up her research on Alzheimer's disease and starting to feel like she had it herself (note to self: take ginkgo), Colin called, wanting to see her.

"I'd like to, but I'm going out with my boss tonight," explained Charlotte. "How about tomorrow?"

Colin ignored her suggestion. "What about after you see him? Why don't you just come over?"

Did he think he could just disappear and then show up and she'd be at his beck and call? That she had no life? Charlotte knew she should just go out with Paul and forget about Colin for a night, but she couldn't. It was what she imagined doing heroin would be like: terrible for you but impossible to resist.

At precisely six o'clock, Paul arrived at the library. He was average height with dark hair, not chubby as Charlotte had imagined. He came over to her and smiled. "Charlotte, finally."

They hugged briefly.

"Let me just finish this memo and then we'll get going."

"Of course—is that the Alzheimer's project?"

"I forget."

He looked at her blankly for a moment and then laughed to show her he got it.

"Sorry, that was a stupid joke."

"No, it's funny."

She introduced Paul to Tom and they chatted about earthquakes while Charlotte finished up her work and sent out a few e-mails.

Later, over dinner at a little Italian place in the neighborhood, Charlotte tried to calculate the earliest time she could leave and go to Colin.

As they were having their appetizers, a Caesar salad for Charlotte and calamari for Paul, she decided that by nine she could be in a cab and speeding toward the Lower East Side.

"It's so good to finally meet you, Charlotte," said Paul, smiling at her.

Charlotte smiled back, feeling guilty.

It was a little awkward at first. She was so used to his on-screen Ix character that it was strange to see him full-sized, not dressed in the robes of a mage. He was wearing light blue pants and a white polo shirt. Kind of preppy, she thought, but it suits him.

"So, Paul, how long are you going to be in New York?"

"Well, I'm meeting with some potential clients, so I thought I'd make a kind of vacation out of it. Spend a couple of weeks, see some museums, maybe a show, do the whole New York experience. Maybe we could do some of it together."

"That would be great, but I'm kind of busy with rehearsals for this play I'm doing."

"Don't worry about it, Charlotte. I know you have commitments. I won't monopolize your time, but maybe I can talk to your boss about you playing hooky from work one day."

"Sounds good to me."

"Any luck with Gorgona?" asked Paul as their entrées arrived. Charlotte had ordered gnocchi with fontina cheese and wild mushrooms. Paul had plain grilled salmon and asparagus.

"I'm watching my cholesterol," he said apologetically. "I've been on a special diet—I've already lost thirty pounds."

"Wow."

"I may have to break down and have dessert, though. Did you see them?" A huge tray of elaborate desserts had just gone by, but Charlotte hadn't given it any notice.

"Yeah, they look great."

"Maybe we could split one."

"My friend Jules says you can't trust anyone who doesn't eat dessert."

"She's very wise."

"Back to Gorgona. No, I haven't been able to kill her. It's incredibly frustrating. I've tried everything. But I do have this kind of new idea about ice arrows."

Charlotte found Paul easy to talk to. They talked Covington strategy for a while and he gave her some good suggestions. He described San Francisco to her, the seals at the beach and the views and the strange fluctuations in weather. In turn, she found herself telling him about her father, the acting classes, what a terrible dress rehearsal they'd had.

"I could never get up in front of all those people," he said. "I don't know how you do it, Charlotte." His praise made her feel urbane and sophisticated, and by the time they had polished off every sticky crumb of chocolate cake and drank every bit of foam from their cappuccinos, she had completely forgotten about Colin and the time.

When they got the check, Charlotte saw the time on the waiter's large glowing sports watch and she couldn't believe it: It was ten. She quickly excused herself to go to the ladies' room.

She called Colin from a pay phone outside the bathroom. He didn't answer. Maybe he went out for cigarettes or was just getting back from his rehearsal. She left a message. "Colin, this is Charlotte. My dinner went longer than I expected. It's ten. I'll call you a little later and tell you exactly what time I'm coming over."

Charlotte put on lipstick in front of the large blurry mirror. She needed this extra layer of confidence to see Colin. It was funny how a guy could make her feel so good physically yet so insecure in every other way.

They walked around the Village. Paul wanted to stop in at a place with a sign that said PIANO BAR. He liked show tunes, he confessed. When they went in, it was like they had entered a bizarre movie set. Men and women, mostly men, were sitting around the narrow dark bar, singing along with the piano player. The song they were singing sounded vaguely familiar, but wrong, as if it were being played on the wrong speed on a record player. After a few seconds, Charlotte realized it was "Hey, Jude," done incredibly slowly with lots of vibrato.

There were two men in their fifties knitting at the end of the bar, singing along to the pianist's rendition of every tune.

"What do you think they're knitting? Secret codes, like Madame LaFarge in Dickens?" asked Charlotte.

"Probably sweaters for their dogs," answered Paul.

Charlotte hadn't known that these kinds of places existed in New York, although she imagined San Francisco as having a piano bar on every corner. She wondered if Paul had a local piano bar he frequented. She and Paul sat down at a little table, ordered some overpriced cognac and listened to the songs.

The piano player started to play some recognizable tunes, some Billy Joel, some Rod Stewart, some Tony Bennett.

Their waiter was very friendly. Every few minutes, he would come over and try to get them to sing. "Come on, you two love birds. How about 'I Got You, Babe'?"

After a while, the waiter started to wear them down. They started humming a little, and finally Paul said, "I'm going to do it."

"Do what?"

"Sing."

"You go, girl," cheered the waiter, coming by at that moment with a fresh round of drinks.

"What are you going to sing?" asked Charlotte apprehensively.

"I'm going to ask the piano player if he knows 'Just in Time.'"

"Know it? Honey, he wrote it," said the waiter.

Paul got up and stood by the piano. His voice was unsteady at first, but after a few bars he started to relax and sing louder and more confidently. By the chorus, the men at the bar were singing along with him.

The song was about finding someone just in time and Charlotte wondered if Paul had a boyfriend. She pictured them holding hands, going to the theater, restaurants, on trips. She wondered if she had found Colin just in time.

When he finished, everyone clapped wildly.

Paul was flushed when he got back to the table.

Charlotte smiled at him. "That was great, Paul. You have a really nice voice."

"I've never done that before. I just thought if you are brave enough to get up onstage, then I should try to do something I've always wanted to do."

"I like that song. It makes you think. I mean, how do you know if someone is right for you?"

"You sound like you're thinking about someone specific."

Charlotte sipped her cognac. "I guess I'm pretty transparent."

"No, not at all. And in answer to your question, I don't know. I'm hoping that you just know. I certainly know that you know it when it isn't right."

"Now *you* sound like you're thinking about someone specific."

"Maybe."

They listened to unique renditions of Billy Joel's "Piano Man," and "I Will Survive" and some nice standards. When they knew the songs, they sang along. There was one statuesque woman who belted out "Quando Caliente El Sol." Until she made jokes about having a penis, Charlotte didn't realize she was a man.

After they had heard "My Funny Valentine" for the third and worst time, Charlotte tried to hide a yawn unsuccessfully. She didn't want to be tired; she was having too much fun.

Paul was apologetic. "I'm sorry, Charlotte, you're probably exhausted and I'm dragging you all around New York."

"No, I'm having a good time, but I guess I am a little tired."

They got the check and Paul hailed her a cab.

"It's not that far," she protested. "I could walk."

"No, take a cab, I'll feel better." Paul kissed her on the cheek and said he'd call her.

After Charlotte got in her cab and saw that Paul was ensconced in the next one, she gave the cab driver the address of Colin's apartment, in the heart of the Lower East Side. She felt slightly drunk and happy.

❦

When the cab driver let her out, she rang the bell of Colin's grungy apartment building.

And rang it again.

And again.

No answer.

It was chilly and Charlotte wrapped her jacket around her, wishing she had dressed warmer.

Where was he? He knew she was coming over. She should have stayed out with Paul or been home in her nice warm bed. This was ridiculous. Maybe he had fallen asleep. She rang the bell again. Then she went to the corner and called him. No answer. Then she called her home phone to see if he had left a message. Nothing.

Finally, she walked away, and then walked back a few times, so if he came by it would look as if she had just gotten there. She was cold and felt stupid and foolish. She had been so looking forward to seeing Colin, being with him. How could he do this to her? Could there be some reasonable explanation, or were the others right about him, that he didn't care about her? Was she an idiot for thinking that he did?

Charlotte walked away for good this time, looking for a cab on the dark, deserted street. She took out her large key chain so she could poke any potential attackers in the eye if she was approached. Or she could use aikido on them, turning their strength against them.

When she got to Houston Street, she started to see signs of life. She felt so cold and tired that when she saw an old Jewish deli she and Colin had met in several times, she went in and slid into a seat at the counter, ordering a potato knish and a cup of coffee.

"Here you go, hon," said the middle-aged waitress, sloshing a little bit of the coffee into her saucer.

"Thanks," said Charlotte, drinking the hot coffee eagerly.

"So, what's the matter, hon? You look like you lost your best friend. It's a guy, isn't it? They do it to you every time."

Charlotte nodded. "He's not there, at his apartment. He's supposed to be there."

"I know the type," said the waitress, refilling Charlotte's cup. "Here, have a rugelah, on me. They're fresh. Trust me. Baked goods, unlike men, will never disappoint you. Anyway, you could use a little fattening up."

"Thank you."

Charlotte felt nourished by the hot coffee, the leaden knish and the waitress's attention, and after a few minutes she went outside, feeling she had the strength to hail a cab and go home.

She remembered things Colin had said to her. *I don't like to be tied down, Charlotte. I need my freedom.* If he wanted to be so free, why hadn't he just left her alone? Why had he called her?

At the loft, there was no message from Colin. She wasn't surprised. He must have totally forgotten about her. It was embarrassing, planning your evening around someone who couldn't care less. The apartment was lit up but quiet when she got in. She heard some soft murmurs from the direction of William's room. He was happy. He had Zoe.

She knew it was crazy, but she still wanted to call Colin, so she picked up the phone a few times and put it down. The humiliation factor was the only thing that stopped her. She had already left two messages. She measured out some valerian and tried to sleep. She lay in bed, songs from the piano bar going through her head as she drifted off. She thought of the song that Paul had sung. *Just in time, I found you just in time, before you came my time was running low.* She thought about Paul—he wouldn't do this to anyone.

In the morning, Charlotte felt angry at Colin all over again. With an extreme effort of will, she waited until ten-thirty to call him.

"Hello," he answered sleepily, innocently, as if nothing were wrong.

"Colin."

"Charlotte." His voice was wary now.

"Yes."

"How are you?"

"How am I? I am not too good. Where were you last night?

"Sorry about the mix-up. Rehearsal went late and then I stopped by the bar and by the time I got back to my flat, it was quite late. I would have rung, but I didn't want to disturb you."

"I went over there. To your apartment."

"You shouldn't have done that, Charlotte." He sounded disapproving, as if she were a small child who had been misbehaving.

"I guess not."

She heard something in the background. "Is someone there?"

"Charlotte, look, can I ring you back? This isn't really a good time."

"Just tell me who it is. Is it Jodee? It's Jodee, isn't it?"

"No, Charlotte, it's not Jodee. There's no one here."

Charlotte felt anger vibrating through her body, out her fingertips, out her mouth.

"Was she there last night? The two of you deserve each other." Charlotte knew she should hang up the phone, but she couldn't stop. "Has she given you your position statement yet? Let me guess: Irish charmer. Well, let me tell you something. Your charm is getting a little tired around the edges, and your accent is annoying after a while. It's *apartment,* not *flat. Pants,* not *trousers.*"

"Charlotte, please."

Charlotte couldn't believe how angry she was. And the more she talked, the angrier she got. "And you drink too much and it's beginning to show in your face."

"What do you mean? What's wrong with my face?"

"Put her on the phone. Whoever it is."

"Charlotte, for God's sakes. You're being absurd. There's no one here, but I really can't talk now. I'll call you later."

He hung up on her. The bastard.

Charlotte put down the receiver as the electronic voice began asking her if she wanted to make a call. No, I don't want to make a call. She looked around the apartment for signs of William. To see if he had heard her tirade. He and Zoe must have gone out—to brunch, probably, or a foreign movie. She didn't know what to do with herself.

She knew she would go crazy if she stayed in the loft alone. What should she do? She had to get out of the loft before she started calling Colin up over and over again to yell at him. Not that he didn't deserve it. Was Jodee really there with him, was it possible that they had spent the night together? She really couldn't take this. She wanted to call him. She picked up the phone, but instead she took a deep cleansing breath and called Paul at his hotel.

"Hi, I was hoping that maybe we could get together if you're not too busy."

Paul sounded genuinely pleased that she had called and suggested they go for a walk.

He said he'd be over to pick her up in half an hour.

Charlotte washed her face with icy water and tried to calm down. She neatened the apartment and made some more coffee. And neatened some more. And paced around, thinking about Colin, trying to hold on to her anger, which was becoming a sharp pain in her chest. How could he just forget about her like that, forget she was coming over? That was the worst part, just not to matter at all to someone.

When Paul arrived, it was such a relief not to be alone with her thoughts. The pain didn't go away, but it was put aside for a while. She talked about her mother and they played Covington and they ended up never leaving the loft to go on their walk. She told him about William and their TV-watching mania. It was such a pleasure talking to someone who actually listened to her, unlike Colin, who always turned the conversation around to himself. She had a feeling that he knew she was upset about something, but was too nice to pry. She didn't tell him about Colin because she didn't want to get upset in front of him.

"I have something to confess," said Paul. "We didn't even have a TV when I was a kid. My parents thought it was the opiate of the masses."

"I thought that was religion," said Charlotte.

"That too. The other boys had *Playboy* magazines under their bed; I had a secret stash of *TV Guides*."

"That's funny."

🙚

William and Zoe came in around five—Charlotte was right, they had been to see a Turkish film and then had Turkish food.

"It was wonderful, so evocative," said Zoe, and Charlotte could tell the film choice had been hers. She looked like she had never watched something without subtitles in her life.

Charlotte introduced Paul to William and Zoe. "This is my boss, Paul—you know, the one I play the game with."

"Ah, yes, the medieval slaying grounds where you conquer evil," said William.

"Right," said Charlotte and they all stood around in an awkward silence.

Finally Paul said, "Maybe we should go out, Charlotte. Do something ridiculously touristy."

"Like what?" asked Charlotte.

"We could take one of those carriage rides in Central Park."

"I don't know, the horses look so depressed," said Charlotte.

"Tavern on the Green," suggested William.

"Too expensive," countered Zoe, "and the food isn't very good. I had a terrible omelet there once."

"How about Chinatown?" said Charlotte, getting into the mood of the thing.

"I know," said Paul, as if he'd just had a revelation from above. "Let's go to a Broadway show."

William and Zoe and Charlotte looked at him, dumbfounded, as if he were talking about going to some exotic foreign event, like snake charming or sword swallowing.

"TKTS—we can get tickets there—I read about it on the plane," said Paul.

"He's right," said Charlotte. "That's exactly what we should do, just go see what's playing, but I'm not seeing *The Lion King* . . . and no Andrew Lloyd Weber."

"Is there anything left?" asked William dryly.

∗

"You don't think we should have invited them to come, do you?" asked Charlotte, feeling slightly guilty as they inched forward on a long line behind people wearing pastel sweat suits.

"No, they seemed pretty happy to be on their own," said Paul.

The streets were jam-packed with tourists and all sorts of people: religious nuts yelling from corners, people hawking cheap T-shirts. If she had been by herself, Charlotte would probably have hated it, but with Paul it seemed kind of fun. They laughed at the people, noticing that the pudgiest people seemed to wear the most serious athletic gear.

When they got up to the ticket window, the only tickets left were for *Cabaret* starring Shannon Doherty and *Tales of the Allergist's Wife* with Valerie Harper.

"We have to go see Rhoda," said Charlotte.

"Okay, Rhoda it is," said Paul, paying for the tickets.

They were starving and snuck Junior Mints into the theater. When one fell down between the seats, they tried to fish it out unsuccessfully, annoying the older couple sitting next to them. They started laughing hysterically as they scraped the errant

Junior Mint from beneath the seat, not caring what anyone thought.

"It's strange. I'm studying acting, but I never go to the theater," whispered Charlotte, still laughing as the lights were going down, earning her a dirty look from the fur-clad matron squished next to her.

The theater was comfortable, and their seats weren't too bad. Charlotte felt safe and protected, as if she were sitting in a plush red candy box.

The play was amusing, one of those stories in which a stranger comes to town and disrupts everyone's lives, leaving the audience feeling happy and relieved when the stranger leaves.

The play was only an hour and a half long, the perfect play length, Paul and Charlotte decided afterward. At the brief intermission, they got drinks at the bar. Charlotte held the drinks while Paul went to the men's room. When he came back, he whispered, "I saw Eric Stoltz in the men's room."

For a moment, Charlotte tried to remember who he was. "Oh yeah, I just saw one of those low-budget movies he was in on cable—*Highball*. It was pretty good."

"I'll make a note of it," said Paul. "I'm always looking for movies to rent." He looked around the room carefully, as if trying to spot other semi-celebrities.

Charlotte wanted to ask Paul what exactly he and Eric Stoltz were doing when he saw him. Women never get to see each other peeing, so it was so strange to think of men standing side by side— she hoped they weren't checking each other out. She tried to think of women Eric Stoltz had dated, but couldn't think of any off-hand—Bridget Fonda, maybe?

When they got back to their seats, they looked for Eric, feeling as if he were a friend of theirs. He was sitting up front with a slim brunette. They speculated as to whether she was just a friend or a girlfriend, finally deciding she was an ex-girlfriend whom he slept with occasionally.

After the show, Charlotte and Paul stood outside Sardi's, looking at the menu.

"We have to do the whole touristy thing," said Paul, opening the door.

They had Caesar salads and crab cakes and shared a bottle of wine.

"So, are you involved with someone?" asked Paul after his second glass of chardonnay.

"I guess you could say that."

Paul looked at her, waiting for her to continue.

"Well, he's Irish. And he's a very good actor. Handsome. Charming."

"He sounds perfect."

"Well, he's not perfect. He's very focused on his career."

"I guess you have to be, in acting."

"And I guess he can be a little selfish sometimes."

Paul sipped his glass of wine.

Charlotte saw herself on the street ringing Colin's bell over and over again. "And he's not always that reliable. And my friend Jules hates him."

"That's too bad, but I hope it works out for you, Charlotte."

Maybe it was the wine, but at that moment Charlotte felt that she couldn't care less what happened to Colin. "I'm beginning to doubt it. What about you?"

"I was in a long-term relationship, but it didn't work out. So I guess you could say I'm available."

As they were leaving, she gave Paul a flyer for the showcase. "If you're still here next Friday, I'd love it if you could come.

You might get a kick out of it. Some of the actors are really good."

"I'd love to see it. Especially your scene."

"Well, don't expect too much. The dress rehearsal really was horrible."

On the cab ride home, Charlotte couldn't remember the last time she had been so silly with anyone. She hoped Paul would come to the show. It would be nice to have someone else on her side.

Unable to sleep, Charlotte went back to Covington. She tried to kill Gorgona, but she kept running out of arrows and getting trapped in a wall of blinding white fire. The fire burned the arrows right out of her quiver. She went back to the blacksmith in town to get more arrows, returned to the dungeons and then got killed almost the moment she entered the room.

Finally, she got the idea to carry extra arrows and hide them in various places around the dark chamber. Then the next time she ran out of arrows she would run into one of the corners of the cavern, pick up more and start firing. Gorgona, she discovered, was too big to fit into the narrow crevices. She went back and forth to town, picking up arrows and reserve parts, healing her magical wounds and hiring troll soldiers to distract Gorgona. Slowly and surely, she was building her defenses.

She kept going, developing a rhythm of getting more arrows, hiding, firing, replacing the troll soldiers as soon as they fell.

Finally, when she felt ready, she just kept her finger down on the mouse and fired nonstop and relentlessly, until she was surprised to see Gorgona's life force begin to drain out of her. Excited, but keeping her calm, Charlotte kept going, firing and firing and firing, until a huge fireworks explosion filled the screen and a deep voice came over her computer speakers: "You have purged the world of an evil force and saved Covington from certain destruction. Thank you."

Charlotte couldn't believe she had actually done it after all this time. She was thrilled. She couldn't wait to tell someone. She picked up the phone to call Jules, but then remembered that they weren't speaking and Jules thought the game was stupid anyway.

Even though it was late, she called Paul at his hotel, since he was the only person who could possibly understand.

"I killed her. I actually killed her."

He knew right away what she was talking about.

"I can't believe it, Charlotte, that's amazing. How'd you do it?"

She described her technique with the ice arrows and the troll soldiers and he was suitably impressed.

"You know, that's kind of the end of the game, Charlotte. I mean, you can keep playing at harder levels, but once you've killed Gorgona, I think that's about it."

She hadn't thought of it that way, but he was right. She had done it, and there was no point going back.

Chapter Seventeen

THE PERFORMANCE WAS starting in an hour and everyone backstage was in full hysteria mode. The floor was dusted white with powder as if fresh snow had just fallen. Most of the actors were in a big communal dressing area, but Heather had scored a tiny closet with a table and makeshift mirror for herself and Charlotte.

Charlotte didn't want to go on. Couldn't face going on. She didn't want to make a big deal about it, but she knew that if she had to walk out onto that stage, she was going to throw up on someone.

"Heather, I'm not feeling too good."

Heather gave her an appraising look. "It's nerves. Remember, it's just those assholes from acting class and their dysfunctional friends and families. Don't sweat it."

That didn't reassure Charlotte. It didn't matter who was out there. It was just the idea of making a fool of herself, the idea of walking out onto that stage at all that filled her with terror. Not to mention the fact that she hadn't seen Colin since that awful phone call when she'd thought he had someone in his apartment with him. She wondered if she had overreacted.

"Do you want me to get anything for you—some water? Is there anybody you want to talk to? Susan? Colin?"

Charlotte shook her head violently. Definitely not Colin. Not Jules. But there wasn't anybody else, was there? Her mother was silent, seemingly gone for good. Her father? What could he do? She didn't know exactly why, but he seemed like the right person to help her. He made her feel safe. "Heather, do me a favor and get William. You remember him, right? He's sitting up front with his girlfriend. But bring just him."

Heather rushed out, intent on her mission.

Charlotte stared into the mirror at her pale clammy reflection.

A few moments later, William rushed in. "Is everything okay, Charlotte?"

She looked at him and burst into tears.

He came over to where she was sitting and pulled up a chair, putting a cautious arm around her shoulder. She grabbed on to him. He put both arms around her and she started to sob.

"What is it, Charlotte?"

"I'm scared," she admitted to his shirt.

"Of course you are, Charlotte. It's only natural. You've never performed in front of people. Especially this many people. Did you see how many people are out there? I think it's a full house."

"Somehow that doesn't make me feel better."

"I'm sorry. Look, seriously, it's okay. Some of the most famous performers in the world get stage fright. Remember that program we watched about Laurence Olivier? He had terrible stage fright."

"I'm no Laurence Olivier. I'm a terrible actress and I won't remember my lines and I hate you."

Charlotte wanted to snatch the words back as soon as they'd left her mouth. But it was true: At that moment she hated him, she hated the fact that she wanted him to be there, she hated him for looking so concerned, for being someone she might start to depend on.

"You hate me?" said William. "Why?"

"For leaving," whispered Charlotte.

"I'm so sorry."

"For what?"

"For everything. For not being there for you. For missing out on you."

At that moment, Jodee pushed her tiny surgically enhanced nose into the room. "Hey, what's going on?" she inquired cheerfully. Heather had just come back into the room and gave her one of her don't-fuck-with-me looks and Jodee quickly retreated.

When anyone else walked by their dressing room and heard the crying, Heather stood outside and told them, "Vocal exercises."

Charlotte cried until she felt like a limp dish rag. She felt like she was crying for everything that had ever happened to her, every humiliation, every disappointment, every abandonment—for Colin, for her father, for her mother. Finally, after there were no more tears left in her, she lifted her head up, looking at William's soaked white shirt, embarrassed.

"Your shirt," she sniffled. "I ruined it."

"It's fine." He smiled and dried his shirt with some paper towels. "You're going to be fine."

She sat down at the dingy dressing table, feeling soggy and bloodshot, but surprisingly better. "How do I look?" she asked.

"You look like a wreck," said Heather, "but it's nothing a little Visine and some makeup can't cure. First put these cold towels on your face and blow your nose."

Heather went to work on her with her bag of makeup tricks.

"You know, Charlotte, you don't have to do the show if you don't want to," said William.

"Yes, she does," said Heather.

Charlotte squeezed more drops of Visine in her eyes. "I know I don't. But I want to. Go back outside, I'll be fine."

William left and Heather said, "Thank God. I was just beginning to think that I wasted a shitload of money on acting classes. Hey, Charlotte, where's that stuff you're always handing out—you know, the emergency-squad drops?"

"The Rescue Remedy?"

"Right. Do you have any on you?"

"I think so." Charlotte rummaged around in her bag till she found the slender vial of brown liquid and handed it to Heather.

"No, not for me, idiot, for you."

Charlotte smiled and put a few drops under her tongue. She thought of the flowers, harvested at midnight, their essences extracted, essences of hope and faith. She could feel it working on her as soon as the bitter drops touched her tongue, spreading calm through her limbs and out to the very tips of her fingertips.

The stage manager called out, "ten minutes till curtain," and everyone was still running around frantically, looking like caricatures of themselves, each feature exaggerated by eyeliner and terror. People were shaking out their limbs as if with palsy, writhing on the floor, emitting all kinds of strange animal noises to get into character. Backstage looked like a zoo or a rave in full progress. Susan finally came by and told everyone to be quiet. "If you're not ready now, you never will be," she said darkly.

Heather and Charlotte waited in the wings in their costumes, nervous and excited. They listened to the other scenes. Everyone was squeezing that extra bit of emotion from every line. In a scene from a Sam Shepard play, one guy looked insane, and actually broke a table during his final monologue. The stage manager cursed under her breath, "Actors."

"Who is he?" asked Heather. "I've never seen that guy before."

"He's that guy that never said a word during our class. They used to call him Silent Joey, like Silent Bob from that movie."

In the wings, the vantage point was crowded from which you could see the famous actor and his famous girlfriend, but Heather squeezed herself and Charlotte in. The famous actor was wearing a silky black shirt and black jeans, looking relaxed, with a little pad and pencil on his lap for taking notes. Every so often he would make little scratches on the pad. His famous girlfriend was sitting beside him, flinging her famous long blond hair behind her at regular intervals, as if she were in a shampoo commercial. She was wearing gray parachute pants and a very low-cut T-shirt, and looked incredibly bored except when the famous actor looked at her, and then she smiled with full wattage.

"She's pretty," said Charlotte.

"So is he," said Heather.

Jodee squeezed herself in next to Charlotte. "That bitch. He said he wasn't bringing her."

"You know him?" asked Heather, incredulous.

"Well, you could say that."

"You slept with him?" asked Charlotte, reading the self-satisfied look on Jodee's face.

Jodee nodded, looking very proud of herself. "He's really sweet."

"When did this happen?"

"Last night. It was great. I was hanging around the studio and John introduced us. One thing led to another."

"I heard they're engaged," said Heather.

"No, that's just a rumor made up by the press." Jodee frowned. She was wearing way too much makeup for Alma and looked like Rebecca of Sunnybrook Farm who had just been forced to work in a brothel.

"I can't believe you slept with him. What about Colin?" said Charlotte, almost feeling outraged on his behalf.

"What about him?" Jodee looked baffled for a moment. "Oh. You thought we were an item. No, Colin's cute and all, but where would that get me? Plus, that stupid Irish girl is always hanging around his apartment."

"What stupid Irish girl?"

Jodee fussed with the buttons on her dress, unbuttoning and buttoning them. "What do you think, two buttons or three?"

"Definitely three," said Heather, smirking.

"What girl?" asked Charlotte.

"Oh, you know, his wife."

His wife? What was she saying? thought Charlotte. How could he be married? She felt nauseated, as if she were going to throw up.

"I don't believe it," said Charlotte. "He would have told me."

"I believe it," said Heather. "And he wouldn't tell you precisely because he wouldn't want to see that disgusted look on your face."

Jodee took out an eyelash curler and started clamping down on her eyelashes. "Well, they don't live together or anything. She's just visiting from Ireland. You know, I think he hates her, but yes, he is married, although whenever I've seen her she's just lying around all day smoking and complaining and eating junk food, which, trust me, she does not need. C'mere, I'll show you."

Jodee pointed to a woman near the back of the theater with limp blond hair and a round face who was probably very pretty once, but now looked kind of puffy and tired.

"Are you okay, Charlotte? You look pale," said Heather, waving a damp cloth in her direction.

"Is that her?" Charlotte asked, looking out where Jodee was pointing.

"You're much prettier than she is, Charlotte," said Jodee, as if that were all that mattered.

"I can't believe you're telling her this right now, before the show," hissed Heather, glaring at Jodee.

"She asked," said Jodee, shrugging her shoulders.

Charlotte and Heather pushed Jodee out of the way to see the woman better.

Seeing her, Charlotte believed that she was his wife. She could imagine Colin and this woman sitting at the pub, fighting, calling each other names, then making up. All the things people told her started echoing in her head, how she deserved better, how he was bad news.

"Speak of the devil," warned Heather.

Colin came toward them and Charlotte turned her head the other way. "Heather, we'd better go up there, we're going on next."

"Good luck," whispered Jodee.

All the new facts about Colin were churning in Charlotte's

stomach and she had that about-to-throw-up feeling again. She took another few drops of the Rescue Remedy and tried to let the calm feeling spread through her.

She smoothed her dress as Susan cued them to go on.

Charlotte tried to remember to experience her *moment before,* like she had been taught. The moment before was about being in character, trying to be in the moment of what the character was doing, before standing onstage in front of all those people. This was to prevent you from walking onto the stage and just standing there like an idiot. Her character's moment before was finding out that her friend Kaye had died and being filled with grief.

As soon as Charlotte got onstage, she felt as if she were having an out-of-body experience. Instead of thinking about Kaye, she kept thinking, Colin is married, Colin is married. She was speaking her lines, but she didn't feel anything. Luckily her lines were right there when she needed them and she remembered where to put her feet.

As she was saying her final speech, Charlotte began to feel that these were no longer lines from a play, but words she needed to say. She thought about her mother and William and Colin and all the grief and regret and bitterness came pouring out of her.

After Charlotte finished speaking, the recorded applause came on and she thought, Thank god it's over. When the real applause started, Charlotte felt tears streaming down her cheeks. Heather grabbed her arm and then they were bowing and walking off the stage and it was really over. She felt drained, relieved, exhausted and happy.

Colin and Jodee were up next. As Colin's character was calling Jodee's character a sexually repressed spinster, Charlotte noticed that Jodee had decided to leave three buttons open on her dress after all, to display a maximum of cleavage.

Charlotte watched from the wings as Jodee upstaged Colin at every opportunity, cutting him off before he finished saying his lines, standing in front of him, forcing him to move out of the way. Charlotte could see he was struggling to maintain his composure and she could tell his rhythm was off. And right before he got to his final speech, Jodee said the wrong line. She'd skipped ahead on purpose, just to trip him up, thought Charlotte. What a bitch. Colin just stood there, out of character, gaping at her, as she pranced around in her little ruffled dress saying her lines. Charlotte felt sorry for him, but then she remembered about his wife. That was who had been there that night she went over. She must have come over from Ireland. Maybe she was the mysterious roommate too.

The last few scenes were good, done by people she had never noticed that much in class. She had been too focused on Colin.

After the last scene, everyone backstage started hugging in an ecstatic frenzy, holding hands, spinning around with relief, as if it were May Day or some pagan rite of actors. Everyone came up to Charlotte and said good job. Since everyone was saying good job to everyone, she didn't give it that much credence. Charlotte felt good about her performance, that she had remembered all her lines and that for a moment she'd actually lost herself in the character.

Charlotte and Heather exchanged presents, a cigarette case for Heather and some red floating candles for Charlotte. "You know, for the bath," said Heather. "If you put them in the bathroom, you'll attract romance."

Charlotte raised her eyebrows. "I don't know about that."

Charlotte was going to get changed when she saw Jules coming toward her.

"Hi."

"I thought you weren't coming."

"I wouldn't have missed this."

They both moved toward each other and hugged.

"I'm sorry," said Jules.

"No, I'm sorry."

"I was an idiot—if you want to go out with Colin, it's fine."

"He's married," said Charlotte, giggling a little hysterically.

Jules jumped back. "Okay, I take that back. I'm going to kill him."

"You were right about him."

"Fucking unbelievable. You were great, by the way. At the end, I even felt a little weepy."

"Wow. Thanks. Stay for the party—I'll be right out."

When Charlotte came out of the dressing room, she saw Colin and Jodee talking in a corner, but they weren't hugging, that was for sure. It looked like they were arguing. Watching him from across the room, Charlotte was still drawn to him, but in a distant kind of way, as if he were a movie star she once had a crush on.

Charlotte went out into the audience to find William and Zoe. They hugged her. "You were wonderful, Charlotte," said Zoe and

Charlotte felt an unexpected surge of affection for her. Paul was there. He had to go back to San Francisco to meet a client, so it was his last night in the city. She had almost forgotten inviting him. He was wearing brown corduroy pants and a blue sweater. He walked over and gave her a cellophane package filled with red roses. "They're not calla lilies, but . . ."

"They're wonderful. Thank you." She introduced everyone to Paul and they made their way over to the office where the prize was going to be awarded.

The twins came up. They were dressed way down in dark turtlenecks and jeans, although they still had spiky high-heeled boots on. Sophie even had some little square glasses on, though Charlotte knew they both had perfect vision.

"Hey, what's the deal with Colin?" asked Lauren. "I thought he was supposed to be such a great actor. His scene wasn't so great. And I thought the two of you were—"

"I don't want to talk about it," said Charlotte. "Let's just say he's ancient history."

The party was nice. The Craft had actually sprung for waiters, who were passing around glasses of champagne and cheese puffs.

Everyone was discussing who was going to get the prize. Everyone suggested someone else should get it while secretly believing they alone deserved it. Charlotte even started to believe for a moment that she would get it.

The famous actor was surrounded like a queen bee in her hive. The crowd parted as he neared the podium to give the prize announcement, flanked by Susan and John. Heather squeezed Charlotte's hand and Charlotte felt as if the two of them were a Russian ice-skating pair at the Olympics, waiting for their scores to come up.

E—— stood at the podium and looked out at them sincerely. "I just want to begin by saying this was a very difficult decision. There were so many wonderful performances and marvelous choices. Each one of you is courageous and you all should be commended for your fine work. Acting is a tough profession. It demands sacrifice and commitment and a high tolerance for rejection." Everyone laughed loudly at this. "Some of you will go on in acting and some of you will eventually choose other roads, but this time spent here at The Craft will inform everything you do."

Out of the corner of her eye, Charlotte could see Jodee preening in the red minidress she had changed into, smiling as if already giving her acceptance speech.

After more preamble and thank-yous, the famous actor said, "And without further ado, the winner of the contest is Joey Fontana."

Jodee looked shocked.

Colin unhappy.

His wife bored.

Heather sounded disappointed. "I guess he deserved it, I mean, he did break a table, but I was really hoping one of us would win."

Joey looked stunned as he walked up to the podium.

Everyone clapped. The famous actor shook Joey's hand. Everyone clapped some more and then went back to drinking.

Later in the party, the famous actor came over and met everyone who had done a scene. When he got to Charlotte, he said, "You did a great job with that part. Good choice of scenes too. I've always loved that movie." She knew he was complimenting everyone, but he really did seem sincere.

Paul heard the comment. "He's right, you were really good, Charlotte. I never knew that you were so talented."

"I like this guy," said Jules, coming up behind them.

"When you go off and become a famous actress, you won't forget us, will you?" asked the twins.

"Shut up, you guys," said Charlotte, embarrassed.

Heather pulled Charlotte away to meet her parents. When she looked back to make sure Paul was okay, Lauren was talking to him, her hand resting on his arm.

Heather grabbed a flute of champagne from a passing tray. "He's cute, in a kind of nerdy-scientist way."

"Who, Paul?"

"I know, at first I thought, oh he's from San Francisco and that he was batting for my team. So I asked him."

"You asked him?"

"Yeah, when you were talking to your father."

"You asked him if he was gay?" Charlotte was shocked.

"Yeah, it's not a big deal. I do it all the time. It saves a lot of heartache. And you will be happy to learn that he is 100 percent heterosexual—he just likes musicals. It's weird, but it's not a crime."

Charlotte tried to make her way back to Paul, but she ran into Colin. She had been hoping to avoid him entirely. He kissed her on the cheek, smelling of scotch.

She couldn't help it, she still felt attracted to him. She thought of what they said in yoga: *You are not your body.*

"You were great, Charlotte."

"Thanks."

"I should have stayed with you. One of us would have won."

If Charlotte had believed for a second he meant that he should have stayed with her romantically, she might have softened toward him, but she knew he was talking about the scene, and was blaming Jodee for his losing the contest.

"Don't you think you should have told me?"

He tried to look as if he didn't know what she was talking about. "Told you what?"

"That you were married. Don't you think that would have added a nice bit of authenticity to your performance?"

"My wife and I . . . it's not . . . we're not . . . it's complicated. . . . I just didn't want to get into all that with you. And it wasn't a performance, Charlotte."

"You should have told me."

"You're right. I fucked up." He touched her arm.

Charlotte thought about times in his bed, the feel of the length of his body against hers, how he used to look at her.

"You should go talk to your wife. She's standing there all by herself."

"All right, all right." He turned away from her and then came back and leaned in to whisper in her ear. "But we had something, didn't we, Charlotte? Something special?"

"Did we? I don't know," she said, her voice without expression.

As he walked away, she didn't turn around to watch him, but she could still hear his voice inside her head and feel the pressure of his hand burning into her arm.

❦

Charlotte walked back to her people. Paul was talking to Sophie and Lauren and she felt a twinge of possessiveness toward him.

He looked up and smiled as she came over.

❦

The famous actor didn't stay at the party long. He was gone before the last tray of champagne made its rounds among the thirsty actors. After he left, the toasts became maudlin.

Joey the winner thanked everyone who had helped him in a kind of lengthy Oscar speech.

"I'd just like to thank Susan and John of The Craft for their dedication and for having faith in me . . . and I'd also like to thank my mother and father and my life partner, Jerome, for his love and support. And I'd like to thank my higher power for never deserting me, even in my darkest moments."

"I wonder if they are going to make him pay for the table," quipped Heather.

"They'll probably frame it," said Charlotte and they both started laughing.

❦

The party began disintegrating. Jodee kept trying to corner Charlotte to complain about that "little shit Joey" getting her part in the movie and how the famous actor had a tiny dick and how his girlfriend used to be a stripper.

"He acted like he didn't even know who I was. Can you believe it?"

239

"Ever hear of karma?" asked Charlotte.

"Karma Chameleon?"

"No, just plain karma, the concept of what goes around comes around."

Jodee looked blank. "You're just upset because I got your part."

"Yes and no. Yes, you shouldn't have taken my part, no matter what Colin told you, and no, because I'm glad I got to work with Heather."

"You were pretty good," said Jodee grudgingly.

"Thanks. I'll see you around."

Charlotte heard her muttering, "Maybe I should change my position statement," as she walked away.

Zoe, William, the twins and Paul all walked out with Charlotte. Zoe and William left first, heading toward Zoe's house.

"Congratulations," said William. "I'm proud of you."

The twins were disappointed they hadn't gotten to meet the famous actor. "She guarded him like a hawk. Oh well, 'bye, Charlotte, 'bye, Paul."

Paul hailed a cab for Charlotte.

As he opened the door for her, he said, "Thanks for inviting me, I had a great time. Your family is really nice."

My family, Charlotte thought. I guess they are. My family.

As Charlotte stepped into her cab, she leaned over and gave Paul a quick kiss on the mouth.

The door shut before he had a chance to say anything. He smiled after her, miming a phone and saying call me.

Charlotte sped home. The loft seemed empty again, but she was glad to be by herself. So much had happened tonight, she needed some time to absorb it all.

Colin was married. Okay, that still hurt, but at least it was final. She would get over him.

She could act. Even the famous actor thought so.

Paul was straight. She had kissed him.

❦

Charlotte, I'm going to miss that game.

Covington? I thought you hated it.

Well, I'm allowed to change my mind, aren't I? Anyway, hate is a relative concept around here. You were good tonight.

Thanks.

It's not surprising. It must be in your blood. You know, I could have been a great actress.

I know. I know.

Corinne?

Yes?

So, are you going to keep coming around?

If you want me to, Charlotte.

Well, I suppose I've gotten kind of used to you.

Corinne sounded relieved. *Okay, but it's only going to be once in a while.*

That's fine. And now, if you'll excuse me, I'm going to take a bath.

I get the picture. You want your privacy, Charlotte. I completely understand.

Charlotte drew a hot bath, filling the bathroom with the scent of lavender. She carefully launched the red candles that Heather had given her until they floated like small boats on a choppy sea. She let herself drift underwater, thinking about William, hoping he wouldn't move in with Zoe just yet. She was actually looking forward to their remaining time together.

2 4 1

Maybe she and William would pick out a dog at the animal shelter and she could walk it in the park. Maybe she and Heather would write a play and it would get produced off-Broadway. Maybe she would visit San Francisco.

She was beginning to think that anything was possible.